VLG – Book Twelve

Vampires, Lycans, Gargoyles

By Laurann Dohner

Graves by Laurann Dohner

Graves is a judge, jury and executioner for the Werewolf packs. Not everyone is suited for the job, but a tragedy in his youth changed him into the man he is today, feared by…well…everyone. So when he completes a job for a nearby pack, and the alpha gifts him with a servant, Graves is shocked. No one in their right mind would make him responsible for another person, especially not an alpha's adopted human daughter. But it's a gift he literally can't refuse.

Her father's alpha position has been challenged, and Brandon, the man who'll likely soon take over the pack, hates no one more than Joni. She has no choice but to seek protection, and to that end, she and her parents have done their research carefully. While Graves might be terrifying, he's also a man of honor. He'll protect her from the new alpha even if it's the last thing he wants to do.

What begins as a rocky partnership soon turns into something more personal. But Brandon has evil plans for Joni, and he'll do whatever it takes—including using people close to Graves—to get her back.

VLG Series List

Drantos

Kraven

Lorn

Veso

Lavos

Wen

Aveoth

Creed

Glacier

Redson

Trayis

Graves

Graves by Laurann Dohner

Copyright © August 2023

Editor: Kelli Collins

Cover Art: Dar Albert

Book ISBN: 978-1-950597-25-3

ALL RIGHTS RESERVED. The unauthorized reproduction or distribution of this copyrighted work is illegal, except for the case of brief quotations in reviews and articles.

Criminal copyright infringement is investigated by the FBI and is punishable by up to 5 years in federal prison and a fine of $250,000.

All characters and events in this book are fictitious. Any resemblance to actual persons living or dead is coincidental.

Chapter One	6
Chapter Two	21
Chapter Three	32
Chapter Four	47
Chapter Five	62
Chapter Six	84
Chapter Seven	97
Chapter Eight	115
Chapter Nine	130
Chapter Ten	143
Chapter Eleven	153
Chapter Twelve	163
Chapter Thirteen	179
Chapter Fourteen	192
Chapter Fifteen	208
Chapter Sixteen	220

Graves - VLG – Book Twelve

By Laurann Dohner

Chapter One

Graves wiped blood off his hands with the towel an enforcer handed him. He'd come to terms a long time ago with being a killer. It was something he did well and the lives he took didn't hinder him from getting a good night's sleep.

The Werewolf he'd just put down deserved death. The body on the ground had housed a piece of shit who'd viciously abused his own mate and killed her younger brother for attempting to protect her.

Worse, the crazy bastard had committed the murder with a shotgun. That was against pack laws. It was legal to own those kinds of weapons but they were only to be used in case of a mass attack by humans. All disputes between pack mates were to be done with claws and fangs. The brother had never stood a chance of surviving such a cowardly, unfair assault.

Graves tossed the bloodstained towel back to the enforcer. "Is that it? I'm out of here otherwise."

Alpha Pete hesitated. "We owe you our gratitude. I'd have killed Jerry myself but he came from another pack. They probably would have declared war on us. We needed someone impartial to deem his offenses death worthy."

Graves understood. "I figured it was that kind of situation when you called Alpha Arlis to ask that a judge be sent here. What pack did Jerry belong to? I'm happy to tell his previous alpha what went down here, and why I deemed Jerry unfit to live, if he has any questions."

"The Gillards."

Graves felt utter disgust but masked it from his features. "I've put down others from Elmer's pack. Just a heads-up, they tend to mate into packs frequently since not a lot of their females survive to adulthood." He glanced at the dead body. "The men were raised to be violent, disrespectful, and abusive to women. To their own kids too, hence not many girls making it to adulthood to become mates. The daughters who do survive that long tend to flee before someone from their own pack mates them. I seriously suggest you warn your unmated women to avoid them from now on. Those bastards tend to have no honor about anything."

Alpha Pete nodded. "My pack has already learned that harsh lesson. Everyone saw what Jerry did to Margie and how he murdered her brother. It was obvious from the moment he arrived that we were going to have issues. I should have denied him acceptance, but his mate begged me to allow him to join us. She truly believed he wanted a better life with us."

Graves avoided looking at the silent woman still sporting bandages and a shitload of bruises, standing near the tree line with her pack. That spoke of how violent the attack on her three days before had been, since Werewolves healed fast.

She'd also just witnessed the death of her mate at Graves's hands. He'd heard that the couple hadn't mated long ago, and he hoped she wouldn't give up on life. It happened with mates sometimes, depending on the strength of the bond. The fact that she'd lost family, too, would make her grief worse.

He didn't ask if they'd had a mate bond or instead made the lifelong commitment in the heat of sex. It didn't matter. He'd done his job. A piece of shit had been judged and executed for his crimes. Only an evil or sick bastard would damn near kill his own mate or use a gun to murder another Werewolf.

"Walk with me," Alpha Pete demanded.

The alpha turned away and strolled toward his cabin. Graves resisted rolling his eyes as he followed. It wasn't required that he obey another alpha, but Arlis would chew his ass if he was flat-out rude. *Play nice.* It was something his alpha said often to him when dealing with others.

Graves fully expected Pete to invite him to join their pack. It wouldn't be the first time he'd gotten that offer. Why pay a high fee to another alpha if they could get a judge to work for a lot less if he lived in their territory? He sighed, tired of dealing with the same bullshit.

They entered the cabin and Alpha Pete waved toward the couch. "Take a seat, Judge."

"I'm fine here." Graves stayed by the door.

The alpha turned to hold his gaze.

"Let me save you some time." Graves crossed his arms over his chest. "I'm not switching packs. Arlis has my absolute loyalty, my family is a part of his pack, and nothing you can offer me will change my mind. You also wouldn't want me here if you knew me well. I'm not the obedient type. Ask Arlis. He frequently calls me a pain in his ass."

The older alpha gazed at him. "I'm curious. Why is that?"

Graves saw no reason to lie or hold back the information. "I'm alpha-blooded. It skipped a generation with my father, since he's pretty mellow, but we joke that I was born with enough aggression for the both of us. I have a younger brother who's mellow too, unless he gets riled. Then it's another story. My dominance levels are probably stronger than yours, so I don't mesh well with many alphas. But I respect the hell out of Arlis. He's a damn good leader who has earned my loyalty and trust."

"There are a lot of good alphas."

Graves gave a cold smile. "Arlis knows I won't follow every order blindly, and he's fine with that. He also doesn't see me as a potential threat to his position. I have no desire to lead my own pack. Most with my dominance level would want exactly that. I'm more of a loner who just happens to live with a pack. I perform judge and executioner duties. Sometimes I'm a tracker. It keeps me mobile, but I know where my home is.

"I'd also never risk joining another pack in case it turns out that I dislike my new alpha. I'd win in a challenge. I'm *that* strong. But I won't risk getting stuck becoming a pack alpha just because some asshole pisses me off until I rip him to pieces. Is that clear enough?"

Graves tensed, expecting Pete to hit the roof with anger. Most alphas didn't like to hear someone boasting that they could best them in a fight...and felt driven to prove otherwise. They tended to have huge egos. He'd had it happen before. Right now, they were enclosed inside the cabin without witnesses. He might hand Pete his own ass, but he wouldn't kill him. Graves really *didn't* want the kind of responsibility leading a pack required. It sounded like a migraine about to happen daily to him.

Pete chuckled. "I heard that about you."

Graves felt uneasy over the alpha's surprising reaction.

"Whispers say that you beat the alpha of the Mellis pack to within an inch of his life and just walked away."

Graves didn't confirm or deny that rumor. It happened to be a true story. The alpha had taken offense when Graves turned down the offer to join his pack, and had tried to force him to submit. It was a huge mistake on his part. One the Mellis alpha had painfully regretted.

He'd left Melvin breathing since he didn't want to own that pack. Graves sighed. "Are we done here? I'd like to get home before dinner. My parents invited me over for steaks. My mother makes these twice-baked potatoes that are to die for and my father is one hell of a grill master."

"Joni? Come out here."

Graves tensed when a door opened down the hallway and a five-foot-four woman walked into the living room. She was a pretty thing; he pegged to be in her early twenties, but that didn't mean much with Werewolves. She could be a lot older. Dark blonde hair fell past her shoulders and big brown eyes peered at him for a split second before she lowered her head, walking to stand timidly beside Pete.

She was also very curvy for a Werewolf, but it was possible that she might be pregnant. It would be odd, though, if the alpha allowed a breeding pack mate to be around an unmated male who didn't already know her. Then again, it might be the alpha's own mate. In that case, it would only be polite to introduce her to the judge who'd just saved them from going to war with another pack.

He inhaled, expecting to verify his guess.

Shock filled him as he realized he'd been very wrong. She wasn't mated *or* pregnant.

She was human.

"This is Joni. Years ago, we got a report of rogue Werewolves attacking humans, and we tracked them down. She was the only survivor. Both her parents and her brother were murdered before we reached their home. They were about to slaughter her for sport." He paused, his expression grim. "She was five years old."

Rage spread through Graves. Some rogues murdered humans just for the fun of hunting something smarter than woodland animals? *Sick bastards.*

"We obviously got to her in time," Pete continued. "But she'd witnessed the brutal deaths of her family. I refused to kill her, nor would I let a Vampire near her to mess with her memories. I also had no idea how humans might have treated an orphan. She was a traumatized child, exposed to our kind against her will. I knew she'd be safest raised by us. My mate and I took her into our home. We were never blessed with children of our own."

Graves glanced at the human again before nodding at Pete. He liked the alpha a little better now. Not all packs would have raised a child from another race, even if it was the right thing to do though. It beat killing her simply because she'd been exposed to the truth of their existence by no fault of her own, or dropping her into an unknown situation with the humans. Even his kind heard the depressing news stories about children raised in the human foster system. The fact that Pete and his mate had adopted her spoke volumes about their compassion and lack of contempt for humans.

"She's been a blessing to us." Pete reached out and placed his hand on her shoulder. "You're a judge, which means you are aware of the laws… I gift her to you as a servant, in thanks for the war you prevented today."

It took a few seconds for the words to sink in. "What the fuck?" Graves snarled, too stunned to remain respectful. "No. I'm not accepting a human servant. That shit hasn't been practiced in forever!"

"It's still a part of our common pack laws and hasn't been banned. I am gifting you with the daughter of my heart. She's full human and therefore can be considered property. Under the law, you must accept my gift. Get your bag, Joni."

The human kept her head down and nodded, turned away, and returned to the room from which she'd come.

Graves's temper exploded. "Fuck no! I'm not accepting a *servant*."

Pete calmly stared at him. "You will, Judge. Under the terms of our pack alliance, you aren't permitted to turn down a gift of gratitude. Joni is now your property. I carefully studied the common laws all packs have shared for centuries. You'll keep Joni safe, feed her, and provide her with a home. In return, she'll cook and clean, and perform any other household chores you deem necessary. As a gifted servant, you're not allowed to fuck her or gift her to someone else."

Graves opened his mouth to cuss the alpha out, but the alpha continued before he could speak.

"I've been challenged. It's going down this Saturday. You want honesty, Judge? I don't think I'll win. I apologize for doing this to you, but I have to ensure my daughter's safety. The upstart who wants to take my place doesn't see Joni as part of this pack or worthy of respect. Her life will become a living hell, if he doesn't kill her outright soon after taking my position.

"I did a lot of research on you. You're honorable, fair, and most importantly, you aren't prejudiced against humans. It's part of your job to kill Weres who abuse women. Even human ones. I couldn't think of anyone better to entrust with her safety."

Graves let all that information sink in. He felt bad for the human's situation, and the alpha's as well, but he didn't want their troubles dumped on him. "I'm the wrong man. Mate her to someone you trust."

"The new alpha would just kill them both. He's made it clear already that he holds no tolerance for anyone who'd mate a human and it will become a death offense. I can't trust anyone from another pack to treat her well, either. You are the only safe option."

"There's got to be another solution."

"I don't agree. It's done. All I ask is that you find her a good home if you ever take a mate, or give Joni her freedom if your pack has learned to trust her before that time. She's loyal to Werewolves. Two rogues may have slaughtered her family but she holds no grudge. Joni's embraced life with our pack. She's as leery of humans as we are."

The human in question returned holding a large duffle bag and a purse. She walked up to Pete, hesitating before dropping her bag to hug him tightly. "I love you, Dad."

The alpha hugged her back and placed a kiss on the top of her head. "This judge will be fair and protect you. I wish you happiness." He shot a look at Graves. "Take good care of my daughter. She's a skilled cook who will serve you extremely well."

Graves let his hands drop to his side, fisting them. "I said *no*."

"The terms of our alliance demand we follow the common laws of our ancestors. If you're refusing, I'll contact the other packs. I'm aware of who Alpha Arlis is aligned with."

Graves quickly debated how badly Arlis would react if he stormed out of there without the human. His alpha would also be pissed that someone had shoved a servant on him, but overall, it could impact other alliances if word spread that they'd broken a term.

That couldn't happen. Their pack was highly honorable.

Anger boiled under his skin as Graves nodded once. "Fine."

Pete kissed Joni on the head again and patted her back. "You were a blessing. Thank you, Joni. Be happy and go with our love."

The human released the alpha, kept her head down, and picked up her duffle bag. She stiffly walked to Graves, stopping in front of him but refusing to meet his gaze.

He growled, "Let's go." He didn't bother to offer to carry her bag. He simply spun, storming outside. The human followed.

He made the mistake of looking back, watching her struggle with the damn bag that was probably heavy for someone so weak. It was large and obviously awkward to hold in one hand by the strap, either way. He stopped and reluctantly took it from her.

She said nothing, but then again, he assumed servants probably weren't allowed to speak unless given permission. Though he really had no clue. He only knew that, in the old days, a pack might keep a captive for a multitude of reasons but it was still extremely rare.

No, not a captive. A fucking servant. The very idea outraged him.

He made it to his SUV quickly, conscious that dozens of pack members hung around, staring.

"Get in the front passenger seat," Graves growled. He opened the back of his vehicle and tossed her duffle into the cargo area, securing the hatch when he was done. He climbed into the driver's side and slammed his door closed. The silent woman next to him put on her seat belt as he started the engine.

He dug out his cell phone and an earpiece, made certain the call didn't route through his Bluetooth connection on the dash, and dialed Arlis. The conversation would be as private as possible.

His alpha answered on the first ring. "How did it go?"

"Death penalty. He was too cowardly to fight fair. The piece of shit killed his mate's brother with a gun for trying to protect her. She's beaten to hell and will have scars. I'd have made him stop breathing forever for that offense alone."

"Fuck," Arlis snarled. "Thanks for handling it. Pete said it would cause a war with another pack if he took the bastard's life. They won't dare come after us."

"Yes. Did he also mention that he planned to gift me a human servant, and used the terms of our alliance to force me to accept her?"

Arlis gasped. "What?"

"You heard me." Graves threw his SUV into reverse, backed out of the parking space and avoided glancing at Joni as he drove forward down the road. He wanted to get the hell out of Pete's territory. "He said I'd break the alliance terms if I didn't accept his *gift of gratitude*. He even threatened to contact other packs to let them know if I didn't take her with me. She's in my SUV now."

"Who the fuck keeps servants these days? Packs in the past used to enslave some humans to prevent them from telling others if they discovered the truth about what we are. It was a kinder alternative than outright killing them. And no Vamp was going to help us back in the day by wiping their memories. Those bastards *hoped* large groups of humans would hunt and murder our packs."

"She was a survivor of a rogue attack as a little kid and raised by the pack. Pete said he's under threat of losing a challenge to someone who would kill her, if said Were becomes the new alpha. He needed someone who would protect her. Tag, I'm it."

"I'm sorry, Graves. I'll have the old pack laws reviewed to see what we can do. Just take her to your place for right now."

He snarled. "That's what I thought you'd say."

"Again, I'm sorry." Arlis did sound remorseful, at least. "We'll talk more when you get back. We'll be all over this to find a loophole."

"I'm out." Graves hung up, glancing at his silent passenger. She kept her head down, her hair hiding her face. "Joni? Look at me." He split his attention between her and the road.

She turned her head and lifted her chin, unshed tears showing in her big brown eyes. He wanted to snarl, hating it when women cried. It made him feel about as useless as tits on a tree. "I'm going to find a way to get you back to your pack."

Her mouth parted but she said nothing.

Strangely, her silence irritated him. "Speak. I'm not an asshole who will strike you for talking without permission. I don't hurt women."

"Please don't take me back to the pack."

She shocked him with the instant request. "What?" Graves couldn't be hearing her right.

"Brandon challenged my father to become alpha. He's been gaining strength and fighting skills for the past few years. It's probable that he'll win if Dad is forced to defend his position to keep me safe. It's best if he steps aside, since I'm now gone. He'll lose his position but at least he'll be alive. I can't go back there."

"So you'd rather be given to a stranger?"

She nodded. "Yes."

Graves wanted to punch something. "That's bullshit."

"Brandon is vicious. He'll kill my father if they fight. My parents and I looked at every option to find me a safe place to go. You were the only choice...I'm sorry."

He let her words sink in. "Your parents discussed this with you?"

"Yes. Of course. They wouldn't have given me to you if I hadn't agreed."

"What the fuck?" His temper exploded as he gripped the steering wheel hard enough to make his claws burst from his fingertips. Graves had to adjust his hold a bit to avoid damaging the leather...and to keep them out of sight of drivers in vehicles high enough to see inside his windows, on the off chance they were looking. "You're telling me that you *want* to be a servant?"

"Not really. But I refuse to let my father die. And very few packs would accept an unmated woman into the fold. None would trust me because I'm human. This was the only way I could leave my pack without being forced to mate a stranger."

She tucked her head again, curling her hands together on her lap. "I'm sorry that you're stuck with me, but I swear I won't be a bother. I'll do my best to be helpful and keep out of your way at the same time. You won't even have to see me if you don't wish. I'll only come out when you're gone, to do whatever tasks you ask me to perform. It's not as if you're home much. You travel a lot. We did our research."

He seethed, realizing the human wasn't a victim after all. She'd agreed to the crazy plan. Hell, it sounded as though she'd had an active part in the decision to be dumped on him. "Why me?"

"You're a judge. As such, you respect the laws and abide by them. Everyone my father spoke to raved about your sense of honor. The other alphas he consulted warned that you aren't the friendliest person, but you're fair. You also have a reputation for being an excellent fighter who always wins."

Her flattery soothed him a bit. "Why is winning fights a consideration?"

"It's a given that some Werewolves in your pack might be tempted to target me because I'm human. They won't act on it knowing I'm under your protection. You terrify everyone."

"*Exactly.*" His temper quickly flared back up. "I'm a killer. You don't want to live with me."

"You don't play with your prey when you're on a job to track and deal with someone who's committed a serious crime. You kill swiftly when it's called for. My father said it shows you have compassion."

Graves glanced at Joni but she wasn't looking at him. "Do you really understand all that my job entails?"

"You are judge and jury for other packs when there's a reason the alpha can't or won't deal with the person accused of a crime. You punish and sometimes have to kill the guilty." She paused. "You also track down rogues who have murdered others. We never learned your birth name, but we know you became known as Graves in your teens because of the high number of kills you've had to make."

He let his claws retract. "That should scare the shit out of you, because it's true."

"I was more curious about why you're called Graves, since it's a known fact that most Werewolves are cremated after death instead of buried."

He glanced over at her. She'd surprised him again. "Seriously?"

She shrugged. "It's a valid question. You don't leave actual graves behind."

"Aren't you worried about being this close to a cold-blooded killer? You're going to be living under the same roof. Has that even occurred to you yet?"

Joni sighed. "You're expecting me to react the way a human would. You take out rogues, lawbreakers, and the scum of our society. It needs to be done. I respect that. It's one of the toughest jobs there is for a Werewolf. You not only do it for your own pack, but those that aren't fortunate enough to have an impartial judge when an alpha needs those services."

She sucked in a deep breath. "If my father had killed Jerry, his previous alpha would have used it as an excuse to declare war, in an attempt to steal our land and wealth. No one will dare attack your pack, which is much stronger. And you have a reputation for being the best judge out there. Not that there are many of your kind. Even if Jerry's old pack takes offense over you killing him, your alpha is closely associated with the VampLycans. The Gillards might bitch and moan but they won't act on it. They'll be too afraid that your alpha would consider it an insult that they questioned his judge, and therefore start a war they can't win. You did my pack a great service. We thank you for that."

Graves kept his attention glued to the road but her words appeased him in ways he didn't like. Few saw his job as she did. Plenty of Weres avoided him, including many of the ones he'd grown up with. They acted as if he'd turn into a rogue one day.

Most humans would scream in terror if they even suspected what he did for a living and run for their lives. Yet here Joni sat, quietly and calmly in the passenger seat, praising him.

The miles passed in silence. Graves had no clue what to do with the woman but she was now his problem. For now, he had little choice but to take her home and give her one of his spare bedrooms.

A damn servant. A human one, no less. Shit.

Chapter Two

Joni kept her fingers laced together on her lap to prevent the big, seething Werewolf in the driver's seat from seeing how they trembled. She and her parents had anticipated Graves not accepting her without resentment. His grumpiness was expected too.

What surprised her was the attraction she felt.

His hair wasn't completely black, like she'd thought from the few pictures of him she'd seen. Brown steaks shone when the sun glinted off it through the window. The color of his eyes reminded her of a stormy sky during the day. They were dark blue with glints of darker gray, the kind that matched his thunderous mood.

Her father had made dozens of calls to other packs who'd had dealings with Graves. They'd learned a lot about him. The judge especially seemed to enjoy punishing jerks like Jerry, Weres who beat their mates or children. It implied he abhorred abusers. She didn't fear that Graves would hurt her. Not even if she made him angry.

The photos she'd seen definitely hadn't prepared her for his sheer physical size. Graves stood over six feet by at least a few inches. Nearly all Weres were muscular, since it was a natural workout to shift forms the way they did. Graves was bigger than most. That showed in his wide shoulders, the way his shirt stretched tight over his biceps and his chest. Even his thighs had the material of his jeans straining a bit.

Just the way he moved as she'd followed him to his SUV hinted that he was dangerous. It wasn't the predatory strut alone, but also how his gaze constantly roamed, seeking a threat. Fully prepared to meet and kill it, too.

That's kind of hot.

She forced the thought away. It would be a bad idea to feel sexual attraction toward her new owner. Scenting her arousal would also probably make him angrier than he already was. That's the last thing she needed, since he was already pretty pissed.

The old pack laws pertaining to servants being punished for angering whoever owned them were clear. At worst, Graves could whip her or lock her up for a few days, but because she was human, any punishment couldn't be harsh enough to cause severe injuries or leave scars.

To earn a more drastic penalty, she'd have to try to escape or attempt to cause him bodily harm. If she attempted either, he was within his right to break her skin, or even her bones.

Sharing the secret of shifters' existence with other humans or attempting to murder her owner were the only things that could get her executed.

She'd never expose Werewolves to the world. Joni believed humans couldn't handle the truth. As for trying to kill him, Graves was the one person most capable of keeping her alive. His death would mean her own. She wasn't an idiot.

"Tell me about yourself," Graves barked after a lengthy silence.

She licked her lips. "I'm twenty-four. Single, of course. One hundred percent human. You heard about how I came to live with my pack." She hesitated. "I'm not sure what else you want to know."

"You don't resent Weres for murdering your birth family?"

It was a reasonable question. "No. Those Weres who attacked us that day were vicious rogues. They killed three human men down the street from us before breaking into our house. That's what had alerted my father. Um…my adopted one, that is. Pete. One of the neighbors had managed to make a call for help before dying. Our pack had infiltrated the human police in town. The—"

"Do you remember the attack?" he interrupted.

"Yes. They broke down the door, grabbed my parents, my brother and me, and dragged us outside. One of them held my mom while the other two ordered my father to run for help. They were laughing, playing with him…said it was the only way to save his family. He didn't make it fifteen feet before the two of them tackled and tore him apart." Joni had told the story before but it didn't get any easier.

"My mother started screaming and collapsed. She either refused or literally couldn't flee when they ordered her to do so. The one who'd been holding her just tore out her throat. Then they told me and my brother to run together. Johnny picked me up. He was ten, and he tried to save me by running as fast as he could. They let him reach the woods before they also killed him in front of me."

"You don't need to say more." His voice came out gruffer.

"But you wanted to know if I resent Werewolves. I don't. Pete and his enforcers arrived during my worst nightmare and killed those bastards, preventing them from tearing me apart next. And don't think I didn't know what they had planned. After I was cornered, my attackers taunted me in graphic detail to heighten my fear. They didn't care that they were terrorizing and murdering children.

"Pete, my adopted dad, held me throughout the entire drive to his house. Sherry, his mate, was waiting on the porch. They spent days taking turns holding me almost nonstop, promising that I was safe, that they'd never allow anyone to hurt me. Though I guess they had little choice; for months after the attack, every time I fell asleep, I'd wake up screaming from the nightmares. They loved me, cared for me, and I learned to love them back. They became my parents."

"I'm sorry that happened to you and your family."

"Thank you. Werewolves and humans aren't all that different. Some are good and others are pure evil. And my adopted father wasn't lying when he said I'm loyal. Yes, vicious rogues killed my birth family, but two amazing Werewolves raised me, kept me safe, and gave me all the love in their hearts, as if I'd been born to them."

"Then why in the hell did they give you to me as a servant? We both know that's a more polite term than the actual reality. They turned you into nothing more than fucking property that I now own."

She flinched at his brutal words. "It's the best that they could do to keep me alive and safe. I'm human. I'm not seen as just another female pack member. It makes everything extra complicated. Do you think your alpha would have accepted me as an unmated woman into your pack? Offered me protection?"

He said nothing.

"Exactly. It's the same with other packs. No one would trust me because I'm human. It wouldn't matter that I've been raised with

Werewolves. They'd be suspicious, maybe think I was a spy gathering evidence of your existence. I'd rather die than betray the packs to humans. Ever watch any of those horror movies about shifters? The only factual parts are that humans tend to attack what they fear or don't understand. Especially when Werewolves are usually portrayed as mindless killers."

Graves grumbled, probably agreeing with her assessment.

Joni continued. It was as if she couldn't stop talking, now that their silence was broken. "At the very least, humans would want to experiment on Werewolves. Try to control them in horrible ways to make them weapons, or steal your abilities to gain faster healing and longer lives. The military. Scientists. Crazy rich people. I could make a long list of the types of humans who'd want to run experiments on shifters. It would be epically horrible if they discovered the truth."

He glanced at her.

"Don't look so surprised that I'd tell it like it is. If nothing else, I'm very honest."

"You didn't answer my question," Graves reminded her. "Why did your father give you to me as a servant?"

"I *did* tell you why. It was the best way to protect a human raised by Werewolves. Dad could have mated me off to some stranger, but who knows what would have happened to me behind closed doors? Some Werewolves wouldn't give me the respect a mate deserves. You just killed an asshole who abused his Werewolf mate. Imagine what Jerry could have done to *me*. And you'd have been called in after he'd murdered me with the very first beating."

She sighed deeply. "My parents didn't want me to end up dead or trapped in an abusive relationship for the rest of my life. Nor did they want me at the mercy of a new alpha who might look down on humans. Arlis isn't like that. Your pack has at least one half-breed that we've heard about, and she's been given a highly respectable job with the pack."

"Are you talking about Shay?"

"Yes. My father learned that she helps your alpha with correspondence. That implies that Alpha Arlis values and respects this Shay, despite her bloodlines. He sees her as a true and trusted member of your pack."

"Shay *is* highly respected by Arlis."

His confirmation proved her point. "Other packs flat-out refuse to accept humans as mates. They order their people to avoid all contact. You opted to belong to a pack that is human friendly."

"If you were aware of our stance, why didn't your father reach out to Arlis to find you a mate with our pack? He could have at least asked before pulling this bullshit."

Joni tried to push down her frustration that Graves didn't seem to be really listening to what she was saying. "As I said, we did our research. While Shay is respected, no one in your pack mated her—and she's only *half* human. The chances of someone wanting *me* are too low to even consider. Dad decided it was safest to gift me to you because you couldn't refuse. Brandon will see it as a human getting the best of him, since I got away before he becomes the new alpha. That's a killing offense, as far as he's concerned. But Brandon won't dare try to hurt me, now that I belong to you."

"You're talking about the guy who's challenging Pete?"

"Yes. Brandon's a year older than I am, grew up with me, but he's always been very vocal about how no humans should live amongst Werewolves. He claims anyone willing to mate and breed with humans is attempting to weaken an entire pack and bring about their destruction."

"That's bullshit."

She agreed, but didn't bother telling Graves. "It doesn't matter. Brandon truly believes it. He encouraged his friends to bully me as soon as I was rescued and brought back to the pack. His hatred of me only grew stronger with time. He thinks anyone with even a drop of human blood shouldn't be trusted. Anyone in our pack who might have befriended me quickly changed their minds after Brandon and his friends threatened to make their lives miserable. They did that to Mincy as well, even though she can shift and inherited all her father's traits. Her mother is human. It's why neither of us have mated to anyone in our pack."

"Did this Brandon and his friends ever attack you?"

"No. My dad always had an enforcer assigned to both Mincy and me, once he realized how much hatred Brandon held for humans, and how quickly it was spreading it to others. It was just…"

"Just what?"

She stiffened when Graves growled the question. "Brandon is desperate to acquire loyalty pledges from potential enforcers, since only two of his friends are strong enough to hold those positions. My father picked eight, since they were also protecting me and Mincy. Brandon thinks he needs just as many as Dad had, so he doesn't appear weak to nearby packs. He's probably right."

"Is this asshole refusing to trust anyone who vowed loyalty to your father?"

"No. Brandon wants to keep all the current enforcers, but three are ready to retire because they're over two centuries old. Three more plan to transfer to family-related packs because they don't like Brandon. After spending so many years guarding me, they've lost all respect for him. Only two current enforcers have agreed to stay on to serve him, should he win the challenge. They're the newest enforcers my father chose. Brandon needs to find four more willing to pledge. He's not above using bribery to gain them. That's when my parents and I began to look at options."

"What kind of bribes did he offer?"

She gut churned. "Brandon promised that under his rule, unmated enforcers will have access to me and Mincy whenever they want. We'd basically have to whore our bodies out to stay alive, since Brandon thinks that's the only thing we're good for. After we're sterilized, of course, because we're not worthy enough to breed pups. Mincy's family found her a mate with another pack just last week. Her parents and younger brother left with her, to be safe from Brandon's retaliation. That left only me for Brandon to use and abuse as he sees fit."

A low snarl came from Graves.

Joni liked that he seemed angry on her behalf. "If I were left at his mercy, Brandon would have made that my reality after becoming alpha. And you can also add resentment to the grievances Brandon and his two best friends hold against me. My father refused to promote them from scouts when they hit maturity because of their loathing of me and Mincy.

There will be no mercy shown when it comes to anyone with human blood in that pack after Brandon controls it."

"Why didn't your father just kill them?"

"They were careful to never break laws. None that would earn that kind of punishment, anyway. And my dad has honor. He would never kill someone just because he doesn't like them. Now Brandon has issued his challenge, Dad must step aside."

"Must? I know you said he thinks he can't win, but I'd rather die fighting than just hand over a pack that I cared about to someone like that."

Joni flinched at his critical tone. "Dad has been ready for years to pass leadership to someone else. He's been declining in health, and sadly, Brandon is the only one who's challenged him in over two decades. He's strong enough to hold a pack together, and he'll be fair to other Weres."

"Won't Brandon be pissed enough to kill your father anyway, once he realizes he gave you to me? He sounds petty enough to want payback once he's alpha."

"My parents are going to live with my uncle Fenel's pack. They'll be safe there, but that pack's also anti-human. It means I couldn't have gone with them. Dad will step aside at the challenge instead of participating in a fight to the death. Brandon will have to allow them to leave. He may be a jerk, but he's not a complete moron. Dad is dearly loved by our pack, and they'd never forgive or respect Brandon if he forced a fight to the death when it wasn't necessary."

"Is Brandon's hatred of humans based on a specific event, or just how he was raised?"

"He's always been paranoid about humans. I don't know how it started. But his hatred for me, in particular, was there from the moment we met. And it became worse after I saved his baby sister eight years ago. He was supposed to be watching her. Instead, he ignored her to flirt with some of the pack girls down at the river, where we go swimming. Beth was three at the time, and she got too close to the river's edge. I saw her fall in, and I ran as fast as I could to dive in after her. I pulled her out, then started CPR when I realized she wasn't breathing. I got her back, thankfully. Brandon was shamed for his neglect, and angry over the fact that it was me who'd saved her." She sighed, remembering the shit-storm that had caused. "It was unforgivable to him."

"What a dick."

"That's Brandon. He actually accused me of drowning Beth to make him look bad, then resuscitating her to appear heroic. It didn't work because there were dozens of witnesses. His own father whipped him in public for making such vile allegations. I can't say I didn't enjoy watching him being punished."

"I don't blame you."

"To be fair, Brandon's not a total dick to everyone. Just to me and Mincy."

"He should be grateful that you saved his sister's life."

"And I'd like world peace and a pet unicorn. It doesn't mean it's going to happen. Wishes are like assholes. Everyone has one. It also means we always have shit to deal with."

Graves snorted. "You're surprisingly funny."

She sighed. "I really am sorry that you got stuck with me. I promise I'll do whatever it takes to make this work in your favor. Free cook, housekeeper...I'll even learn to help you with your job, if you'd like."

He didn't respond.

Joni inwardly winced. His mood may have mellowed, but Graves wasn't going to easily accept her new role in his life. It didn't come as a surprise.

Chapter Three

Graves kept his lips firmly sealed as he watched the short human inspect the interior of his cabin. Joni kept quiet too. Her expression didn't show emotion at all. He wondered what she thought about his home. It was a little too big for him, with three bedrooms and two bathrooms, but the location was close to family so he'd claimed it.

She entered the kitchen and paused before facing him. "May I?"

"May you what?"

Joni finally met his gaze, peering at him with her big brown eyes. "I'd like to nose around to see what I'm dealing with, since I'm taking over the cooking. How do you want to handle that? Do you want to provide a weekly menu of what you wish to eat every day, and then I make a grocery list of ingredients I'll need? Or do you want me to go grocery shopping? I can cook almost anything. I'll need to use your SUV if you send me on errands, though. I have a valid driver's license."

Shit. He hadn't thought of any of that.

"I ran errands for the pack but I used one of the community vans. There was never a reason for me to have my own personal vehicle. Dad and Mom didn't allow me to enter any of the human towns without at least one enforcer, and even then only to pick up supplies for the pack house."

"Why the protection in town?"

"I learned how to fight to defend myself, but I'm not a Were." She gave him a smirk. "My parents were a bit paranoid about my safety. I didn't need guards when I was away from Brandon and his friends, but they worried about crazy humans, too. Ever watch the evening news? My parents did. A lot. They thought a human man might abduct me if I drove alone."

He allowed his gaze to roam over her, from her small black ankle boots to the top of her head. "What do you weigh? About one-twenty?"

Pink tinged her cheeks. "One-thirty-seven, master."

Graves stiffened. "Why would you call me that? *Don't*. I'm not a fucking Vamp."

She tucked her chin down. "Sorry. I've studied the rules of being a servant. I must answer all your questions and address you by the proper title. There are just some questions I don't prefer. Anyway…how would you like me to address you?"

"I weigh two hundred and sixty-six pounds. What's the big deal about weight?"

Her brown gaze met his briefly. "It's a woman thing."

"Whatever." He sighed. "Use my name. I went grocery shopping a few days ago. There's a ton of food. I'm also not picky about what I eat, but I have a big appetite. We'll work out the logistics of this mess later. For right now, make yourself at home. Get to know the place. I have somewhere to be." He spun and walked to the front door before glancing back. "There's a small guest bedroom downstairs and a larger one upstairs. Take your pick. Just stay out of my bedroom. That's off limits to you. Understand?"

"You don't want me to clean it? Make your bed? Do your laundry?"

"No. Stay out of my bedroom. I'll be home in a few hours. Feel free to eat without me."

"Do you want me to make your dinner?"

"Not tonight. And don't go outside, either. No one in my pack knows you yet. You'll be safe inside my home." He left, closing the door behind him before she could ask him more questions.

Graves headed toward his parents' place. He'd decided to walk instead of driving; they didn't live far and he could use the fresh air to think.

A fucking servant. He still couldn't wrap his head around it. Financially, he could afford to support the woman. A human especially, since she probably didn't eat much anyway. Joni seemed on the small side of average to him.

It was having her underfoot, sharing his personal space, that would annoy him. He'd lived alone since he was a teenager.

He picked up a scent and changed direction, meeting his younger brother, also walking to their parents' home. Micah stopped on the path and waited for him to catch up, offering a grim frown.

Graves sighed. "You heard?"

"Yes. Arlis shared the news that we have a human in our territory and she's under your protection. What was that alpha thinking, giving you a woman? I didn't know any packs kept human servants anymore. That screwed-up shit stopped happening like a hundred years ago. At least."

"Tell me about it. Here's the real kicker. She was in on the decision to be given to me. The alpha couple treated her like a blood daughter. They had her permission to gift her as my servant."

"Why?" Micah scowled. "Do you think it's a setup? That she'll try to slit your throat while you sleep? You've made a lot of enemies."

Graves snorted. "Wait until you see her. A pissed-off squirrel could kick her ass. I'm being used all right, but it's because she needs a bodyguard, and someone to feed and house her."

Micah shook his head. "Is she fuckable?"

"It's against the rules."

"That's just cruel! If I were forced to have a woman move in with me, I'd fully expect to get laid for my trouble."

"Dickhead."

"Honest." His brother shrugged. "Arlis is having Yasha review the old laws to see if there's a way to fix this. We'll get the human out of your home. I take it you didn't want to bring her to dinner?"

"No. I needed some space to cool off."

"Is she that hot?"

"She's not my type. I'm just furious to be put in this position."

"You fuck humans occasionally. It's rare, but I know you have."

"She's too submissive, and she was in on the ridiculous plan to trap me." Graves sped up his pace. "Do Mom and Dad know?"

His brother kept up easily. "Yes."

That was the news Graves dreaded. "Fuck."

"*Everyone* has heard. Like I said, Arlis announced it. You're the talk of the pack once again. Only this time it's not for who you've killed or how many."

Graves flashed his middle finger.

Micah chuckled. "You know you're going to get a lecture from Mom. Don't be surprised if she offers to take the human off your hands. She's always wanted a daughter."

"I'd pass her off to someone else in a heartbeat, but Pete said I wasn't allowed to give her to anyone or free her until I take a mate. He obviously schooled himself well on the ancient laws, so I'll take his word for it."

"Shit! You're stuck with this human forever? What's her name?"

"Joni."

Micah cracked up, highly amused. "That's a sweet name. It sounds very tame compared to yours."

Graves wanted to punch his younger brother but resisted. Nothing about this situation was funny. His parents' cabin came into view, their mother already waiting on the porch. He saw her expression and knew his day was about to go from bad to worse.

His brother just *had* to mutter the obvious. "Mom's not happy with the whole servant thing."

"Neither am I."

"Tell me it isn't true," his mother stated as they drew closer, crossing her arms over her chest.

Graves stopped in front of her. "Don't give me that look, Mom. I didn't ask for this bullshit. I was either say yes, or cause Arlis trouble with the other packs. Of course I don't *want* a servant. And I sure don't want a woman living under my roof."

His mother pursed her lips. "I'm glad you said 'woman' instead of 'human.' I adore Gerri."

Graves nodded. Everyone loved his cousin Wen's mate. "Her being human isn't the problem."

"Why isn't she with you? I want to meet her."

"I needed to get away from her for a bit," he admitted. "I'm *pissed*, Mom."

"Oh, Graves. It's not *her* fault." Tears filled his mother's blue eyes.

His guts clenched. Graves hated to see her cry. "It kind of is. She admitted to agreeing with her parents' decision. She was actually part of it. There's some jerk in her pack who's going to challenge the alpha. They felt she'd be safer with me instead of staying there. The soon-to-be alpha isn't human friendly."

When he reached the porch, his mother changed her tense stance, reaching out to rest her palms on his chest as she peered into his eyes. "She *will* be safe. You'd never hurt a woman. I raised you right."

He couldn't argue with that. "You did."

"I want to meet her. I also think it would be best if she moved in here with us. I love you, but you're probably terrifying the poor girl. She's going to need a bit of time to realize that you aren't anything like the rumors she's probably heard, Graves."

"I can't do that. Trust me, I wish I could send her over here, but it's apparently against the rules. I have to let her live with me, remaining under my protection."

"Bullshit. Who's going to know?"

He arched one eyebrow. "Who *isn't* aware that she's here, Mom?"

The front door opened and his father ambled out with a grin on his face. "A human, huh?"

Graves bit back a growl. "Don't even start, Dad."

"Come on. It's funny."

"Angelo," his mother snapped, turning on her mate. "Don't make me hurt you."

His father stepped back, hands going up. "Don't hit me, Mandy. I surrender." His father grinned wider. "But it's Graves. You'd expect *Micah* to end up in this situation. He's the soft-hearted sap."

"I love you too, Dad." Micah scratched his chin with his middle finger. He dropped his hand fast when their mother spun around to shoot him a dirty look.

"I just mean *anyone* is softer than Graves," his father chuckled. "Love you too, son."

"What are we going to do?" His mom put her hands on her hips. "We need to make sure this girl feels welcome and accepted. She's all alone in a new place. I bet she's scared." She zeroed in on Graves with that motherly look he knew too well. "You should have brought her. She needs support and love. What's her name?"

"Joni."

"How old is she? I want to know everything about her."

Graves sighed. Maybe coming to dinner with his parents hadn't been such a good idea after all. His mother would likely never stop asking questions about the human who'd invaded his life and his home.

* * * * *

Joni unpacked her duffle bag, relieved that Graves had hangers in the empty closet. She reached up to wipe away her tears as he worked. As angry as he felt over being tricked into taking her with him, it sucked for her too. He resented her, hadn't been shy about his feelings, but she'd given up the only family she'd known for years.

She knew there was no use crying about it. She'd done what was necessary. And Graves didn't have to like her; as promised, she'd make herself useful and stay out of his way.

A quiet buzzing sound came from her purse on the bed. She hurried to pull out her cell phone and smiled when she saw the name on the screen. "Hi, Mom."

"Are you okay, baby? Is that Graves still angry?"

"He's fine." Joni took a seat on the queen-size mattress. "There's going to be some stress to deal with. We expected that. He's not happy about me being in his life, but he took it better than I imagined."

"Is he treating you well?"

She glanced around. "You could say that. The spare bedroom is nice and it has a private bathroom attached."

Her mother made a small sighing noise. "Good. I was afraid he'd stick you on the couch or give you a mat for the floor. Some Werewolves can be real pricks."

"We did our research well. Graves is super close to his family. People respect him. He hates abusers of women and kids. I told you that he wouldn't treat me as if I'm a pet."

"I still worry. He kills for a living."

"He can keep me safe and no one would be stupid enough to mess with him. That's all that matters. We've been over this."

"I know, but this is difficult for me. That's why I couldn't be here when you left. I knew I'd cry."

Me too. Joni forced a false cheerfulness into her voice. "It's going to be fine. You and Dad can retire. You'll love spending more time with him, now that he'll be done running the pack. He's still going to step aside, right?"

"That's the plan."

"Good. Will you promise that you'll let me know how it goes?"

"Of course. I'm already packing what we plan to take. I just wish you were here."

"Me too, but this is for the best."

"Is it? You're my baby. I keep thinking about all the bad things that could happen to you. Has that Graves hit on you? Molested you?"

"No! Of course not."

"Remember, it's against the law for him to touch you. You're not a sexual outlet for this prick to take advantage of. Weres are super horny."

"Geez, Mom. Please spare me the Werewolf sex talk." Joni had heard it a thousand times. "Graves is honorable. Besides, he's already avoiding me and he'll rarely be home. He travels a lot, remember."

"But *you* might become attracted to *him*. Just don't invite him into your bed, Joni. It will be a mistake if you void the law by giving him permission."

"Mom…not this again."

"Werewolf males can seduce anyone if they set their mind to it. I don't want you getting your heart broken or his future mate deciding your stuffed head would look good over his mantel. Some mates might find it upsetting if he's slept with the servant he's responsible for and issue a challenge when he brings her home, since you already live there. She could see you as a threat and hate you for sharing his bed first. It would be the alpha's decision if he allowed a fight between a Were and a human under those circumstances. I doubt Arlis would allow it, but it's not worth the risk. You're stuck in that pack now."

"We discussed all this before."

"Did you pack your vibrator?" she asked, ignoring her protests.

Heat flushed Joni's cheeks. "I'm so uncomfortable with this conversation right now. Please make it stop."

"Never masturbate or use your toy when he's home. He'll smell you. Meet your own needs when he'll be gone for at least a day. Shower right after. Wash your sheets too. Air out your bedroom to make sure the scent of arousal doesn't linger—"

"I *know*. Werewolves have great noses. I might not have one, but I can never forget that you do. I'm also aware that he's got super-hearing."

Embarrassing memories flashed through her mind. Her mom knew about her vibrator because at one time, Joni *had* forgotten that not only could Werewolves smell arousal, they had exceptional hearing. Talk about emotional trauma. Her mom had confronted her about it at breakfast the very next morning, suggesting Joni not use it while her parents were home.

It hadn't mattered that her bedroom wasn't near theirs. They'd still heard it. She's also learned not to read sexy books around her parents. They picked up her physical reactions by smell anytime a particular scene turned her on. She'd been mercilessly teased by them both, more than once.

"I know humans can have strong sex drives. Just don't invite him to break the rules. That's the only way he can touch you."

"Mom, please," she begged. "Stop!"

"It needs to be said, Joni. We reduced you to servant status. It hurt us to do so, but the harsh facts are that, under the written common laws, you don't have the same rights as a Werewolf. Your life is indentured to him. And a pregnancy would be disastrous. He wouldn't have to mate you, and if your pup carries the shifter ability of the father, he'd most definitely take it from you. The law is on his side, regardless if you're the mother. Do *not* encourage him in any way, Joni. Please don't. It's not worth the risk."

"I'm not going to give Graves permission to void the rules, and I sure won't get pregnant. I don't even enjoy sex, Mom."

Her mother was silent for a beat. "How would you know?"

"Because I'm not a virgin." She hated to admit that to her mom, but doing it over the phone helped.

"What? Who? When? None of our enforcers were allowed to touch you! They're the only males we allowed near you. Who broke the rules?"

She bit her lip. "It wasn't any of them. You sent me to a human high school, remember? I had a human boyfriend."

"*You what?*"

Joni flinched at her mother's enraged snarl. "Calm down. I was just curious, and I sure couldn't have sex with someone from the pack. It was right after graduation. Remember that party I went to, when I snuck away from my guard? It wasn't the best experience."

Her mom still sounded angry but her tone was calmer. "Did a human boy hurt you?"

"No. I mean, it hurt. I'd read that sometimes happens the first time. We did it twice, but the second time wasn't great either. It didn't do much for me. I shower afterward to prevent you from finding out, before I called my guard to tell him where I was. Trust me, I'm over the whole sex thing. My vibrator is way better. I don't need a man."

"You slept with a human. That's a totally different experience. Be wary of that Graves. Werewolves are much better at sex."

"It's just Graves. Not *that* Graves. And how would you know that Weres are better? You've been mated to Dad forever."

"We had to blend in with humans to avoid suspicion back in the old days. I was nearly three decades old before I met your father. That means

I had a life before him. I slept with a human as well. It wasn't all that pleasurable."

That shocked Joni. "I didn't know. You never said anything."

"Werewolves are much better in bed than humans. This Graves could seduce you easily. I fear for you, baby. He's an attractive Werewolf. You're right under his nose now. You must stick to the rules by not giving him permission to touch you. It's the only way to avoid getting hurt. Werewolves as strong as him are always drawn to their own kind. He'll only use your body, then discard you when his real mate comes along."

"I hear you." It was a sad fact of pack life. At twenty-four, Joni had seen plenty of pack couples break up when one of them found their mate. The unlucky half of that previous pairing suffered heartbreak and sadness over watching their lover bond forever to someone else. It just proved how tragic things could turn in a relationship that started based on sex.

"Good. I'll call you after we confront the challenger."

Joni smiled at how her mother often refused to say Brandon's name. It was a clear insult to him. "Be safe and well, Mom. Give Dad my love." She disconnected, wiping away the last of her tears.

No one from her pack had wanted to mate her, and it hadn't just been because of Brandon. He'd dissuaded them, sure. The threat of being bullied was always present. Mostly though, she knew the males hadn't seen her as mate-worthy.

She couldn't shift and run with them in the woods. The chances of her children being able to shift were fifty-fifty. It was a risk no Werewolf wanted to take. They wanted their children to be born strong-blooded with all the same traits of their kind.

"Damn it," she sighed, laying on the bed and staring at the ceiling.

Rogues had changed the path of her life when she was a small child. There was no way she ever wanted to try to blend in with humans again. They were too foreign to her now. Just going to a human high school had been hellish, every single day. She'd been raised too differently from other students to ever fit in or think the way they did. Yet, her parents had insisted on sending her there to learn about her people.

No. She'd spent plenty of time with humans for those four years, and she wasn't overly impressed with her own race and their thought processes.

Graves was a prime example. One of her human friends from high school would have felt he deserved to spend the rest of his life in prison for the things he did for his job. Not her. Graves was a hero. He might kill, but he took out bad guys who didn't deserve to live.

She hadn't admitted it to her parents, but the more she'd learned about Graves when they'd gathered their research, the more determined she'd become to belong to him. No one else could offer the level of protection he did.

Okay, the fact that he happened to be hot had factored into it a little. Graves was very easy on the eyes.

What if he *did* hit on her? Would she remind him that it was against the rules or give him permission to touch her? Despite what she'd promised her mother, she wasn't at all certain, now that she'd seen him in person. Photos hadn't done him true justice. He'd gone from good-looking to super-sexy.

"Damn," she said again, closing her eyes, his image instantly appearing in her mind. Graves had a rugged, masculine face. It wasn't handsome in that fashion model way. He had more of an "I'll kick ass if you look at me wrong," bad boy sex appeal. Those bluish-gray eyes of his were something she liked, too. The dark hair and his tan skin really made the color pop when he looked at her.

Then there was his body. His height and muscle mass should have turned her off, since she'd always been attracted to a different body type. The human she'd slept with had been fit but lean. Like a dancer or swimmer. That was the type she'd liked best.

Past tense. Graves did it for her now.

"I don't want my heart broken. I'll stay strong," she whispered aloud. It could never end well for them, even if he somehow found her attractive. He'd prefer a Werewolf over Joni any day of the week. Strong Werewolves were drawn to the same. He'd probably end up with a female enforcer type. Vicious, deadly, and just as muscular.

A human with love handles could never be *his* type.

Chapter Four

"Tell me some good news." Graves gave Yasha a pleading look as he entered her home later in the evening, after dinner with his parents.

She had to be over four hundred years old, if she was a day. He liked her best out of all the elders in his pack. Yasha was the wisest, as far as he was concerned. It wasn't just that she'd survived all those centuries, able to give solid advice to anyone who needed it. She was also a bit of a scholar. He dealt with her most often when he had to go over the ancient pack laws regarding questions for his judge duty. She was their expert on the subject.

"You're currently fucked," Yasha muttered, pointing for him to take a seat at the bar in the corner of her living room. She moved behind it, pulled out a bottle of whiskey, and poured the liquid into two glasses. "You're stuck with the servant for a while. The only current good news is that with time, the pack will learn to trust her unless she's a twat. Is she?"

"I'll assume you mean unlikeable or someone who would turn on us. I think she'll do fine here. Joni loves her adopted parents and seems loyal to our kind, more so than to humans."

Relief flashed in her eyes. "Loyalty to our kind is damn good. Especially since I just said you're stuck with her for a while. Drink this." Yasha pushed the whiskey at him.

He lifted the glass and took a sip. "What's *a while*? I can't just set her free?"

"You can when the pack trusts her, and only if Arlis agrees to give her pack status despite her being a human. Nobody knows this woman. There's also a host family clause in there for unmated females when she becomes part of our pack, and I know your mother. Mandy will take responsibility and claim a human as family. Take her around, introduce her to everyone, and maybe in a year, you can change her status. Arlis will very cave in that time, with you snarling at him constantly."

"A year?" He downed the rest of the booze in the glass and held it out for more. "Unacceptable!"

Yasha finished her own glass and poured more whiskey for them both. She lifted hers. "I do like you, Graves." She took a sip and grinned. "But you *are* fucked. And you can be in the literal way, as well. I figure sex is the least you should get out of this deal, since you're stuck with a human living under your roof."

He gaped at her. "Are you hitting on me?" He felt a bit horrified. Yasha didn't appear anywhere near her actual age, maybe a good-looking mid-fifties in human years, but he'd known her all his life. She was like family.

"Hell no!" She threw back her head and laughed. "That's a riot! I have great-great-great-grandsons older than you." She met his gaze with a smirk. "I'm a Were, not a cougar. I'm talking about your human. Here's the thing—the original laws strongly discourage our males from mating with humans to keep our bloodlines pure, despite the fact that extinction of our race was our biggest worry way back when. Especially before things like phones and the internet were invented. Most shifters had no clue if other packs were surviving at all, unless they literally ran into each other.

"Every pack assumed they might be the last of our kind. And they'd literally rather die out than dilute the bloodlines. So it was forbidden for unmated males to seduce servants without their alphas' express permission. Humans who knew the truth, of course, were terrified of our kind. They compared us to pure evil. The idea of being fucked by one of us? That was probably the root of their nightmares for *any* servant."

Graves snorted. He recalled hearing one of the elders tell a story from her youth, when she'd been accused of being a witch. She'd been the only survivor of her small pack and had lived amongst humans. The townspeople had planned to drown Victoria, but she'd managed to escape by shifting to get free of the ropes that bound her. She'd had a human husband at the time, and he'd tried to kill her when she'd begged him to flee, fearing the repercussions of marrying a woman he'd always known was a Were.

Victoria had kicked his ass and left him unconscious in their home. While on the run, she'd met her Werewolf mate and joined his pack. Sharing the story was her way of proving that, even through bad times, good things could happen.

But for Graves, it was proof that not *all* humans were terrified of Weres.

Yasha, unaware of his thoughts, smiled. "Right? Like we were Satan himself. Humans weren't going to agree to fuck an evil, vile thing. The lawmakers knew it. But the same law that protected the bloodlines, *also* stated that widowed men are exempt. They were allowed to seduce their servants if they'd lost their mates. Our own women would have avoided hooking up with a male with a broken bond, unless the pack was dying out and pups were desperately needed to prevent extinction. In that case, all Weres would have been ordered to breed, regardless of the ability to bond as a pair."

He frowned. "I'm not a widower."

Her gaze narrowed. "You are under *our* laws."

He tensed in his seat.

"You met your mate, Graves. Knew Londa was yours...but she died before you both reached the age of consent to claim her. Not that the actual claiming matters. You both acknowledged the coming bond and planned to seal it when the time came. Under the law, you're considered widowed."

Shock rendered him silent.

Sadness flashed on Yasha's features as she reached out, placing her hand over his. "I can read the written words to you if you require proof, but trust me...it states any male who loses their mate and takes a servant may bed her. Males wrote those laws, of course. It gave them the opportunity to have companionship. A servant in their bed was better than no woman at all. We're sexual creatures."

He lowered his gaze to his drink. He hated when anyone brought up that part of his past, but he understood it was relevant to what the elder was saying.

Yasha released him. "You might be stuck with this human for a year or so, but you've got yourself a bed partner anytime you're in the mood. Just don't knock her up. Arlis would ask you to mate her for the child's sake. He's a compassionate alpha who'd want that pup to have both parents."

She studied him when he remained silent.

"I thought the news would please you. Is she ugly or something?"

"No." He still didn't look at Yasha.

"Too young? I heard she was at least twenty-something."

"She's old enough. Just not my type."

"That's the only good news I have for you, I'm afraid. I truly thought it would cheer you up."

"It's...something."

She snorted. "Most men would be happy. You're responsible for feeding and housing her, keeping her safe, beating anyone's ass if they look at her wrong. The least you should get out of it is fucking privileges. You're legally allowed."

He jerked his head up suddenly, and grinned. "I'm sure she'll be thrilled to hear that."

Yasha cocked her head in question.

"That's the answer to my problem." Graves put down his glass, leaned forward, and grabbed her face with both hands to plant a kiss on her forehead. "You're as amazing as ever!" He released her. "I'm going home to let her know."

Yasha appeared surprised by his response. "Are you *that* excited about fucking a human?"

"Just the opposite. She's going to flip the hell out." He stood. "Thank you."

"You're sounding a little insane, Graves. I think you should probably take a vacation from your job soon."

He chuckled as he left Yasha's house and ran all the way to his cabin. The lights were on when he let himself in but his little guest was nowhere to be seen. He sniffed the air, following Joni's scent to the downstairs guest room, and knocked on the closed door.

She answered by cracking it open about an inch, peeking out at him with one eye. He glanced down but couldn't see her body, since she was mostly hidden behind the door.

"I took this bedroom. Is that okay?"

He didn't want a door between them for this conversation. "Get out here. We need to talk."

She hesitated.

"Now. That's an order."

"I...I didn't think you'd want to see me any more today. I put on my nightgown. Can I get dressed first?"

"No. Out here *now*, Joni." He harshened his tone to let her know he meant business.

She opened the door slowly, and he took in the sight of her wearing a jersey-style oversized shirt. It was blue and white. Matching striped socks with those same colors adorned her small feet. She'd pulled her hair into a messy ponytail on her head. He also spotted a book on the bed, proof that he'd distracted her from reading.

He backed up, motioning her forward.

"Did I do something wrong? I made a sandwich but I cleaned up the mess."

"You didn't do anything wrong." He turned and strode into the living room.

She stopped by the back of the couch, keeping it between them, probably trying to hide her legs. He'd already observed they were shapely. He hated that he'd noticed, but he was a male. He'd also noted she looked cute as hell and innocent in a sweet, sexy way.

He didn't like any of those qualities in women, and he harshly reminding himself of that fact.

"I had a discussion with one of our elders. Yasha is my main advisor. I consult with her when I'm unversed on unusual laws the past elders wrote for universal pack procedures. She's probably the most versed on ancient pack laws of any elder I've ever met."

She paled slightly, clutching at the leather cushions along the back of the couch.

"Curious now?"

She licked her lips. "You found a way out of this, didn't you?"

He studied her face. Emotions flashed across her features that he easily identified. Dread and fear. She paled even more.

Part of him was overjoyed to see it. She and her parents deserved it for what they'd done to him, making her his servant. Like he needed that bullshit. He didn't.

He smiled when he finally answered. "Yes."

"That's not possible."

His mood grew somber as he considered his next words…how to bring up a painful topic. "What do you know about my past?"

She bit her lip, her fingernails digging into the leather as she clutched harder at the couch. "I don't know what you're hoping to find out. Just tell me."

"Our pack used to be led by Arlis's parents. We were attacked by another pack, making Arlis our alpha when his mother and father died."

"I'm aware of that. It's why you became a judge and tracker. You seek vengeance against those who take innocent lives. Another pack attacked yours in the middle of the night without warning, trying to steal your territory. It was completely dishonorable and against pack law."

"Yes. One of those innocent lives taken during the attack happened to be my mate." He lowered his voice, hating that he had to share that information with her. Hell, he hated to even *think* about what he'd lost during that attack.

"You never had a mate. We checked."

"I was never able to claim her. We were both under the age of consent. She was only fourteen when she died, two years my junior. I never even kissed her."

"How did you know she was your mate if you were so young?"

"Pure instinct. I just...knew. So did she. It happens sometimes."

Joni's breathing increased but she tried to appear calm. He wasn't fooled. Sheer panic showed in her eyes now. They stared at each other for a good minute before she finally spoke.

"You never actually mated though. I'm very sorry for your loss, Graves. Truly. I can't imagine your grief. Are you telling me that you'll never claim a mate, and it means you won't be able to free me one day to become a member of this pack?"

After a beat, Graves decided the threat of never being free might work just as well. He'd never even have to mention the sex thing.

"I won't take a mate since it wouldn't be fair to any woman, knowing that I was supposed to bond with another. She'd have to settle. That's never going to happen with my job. Only a fated mate would want to lock her life to someone who kills as often as I do. Now...are you ready to call your father to end this farce? Pack your belongings. I can drive you home as soon as you get dressed."

She lowered her head, breaking eye contact.

Graves frowned. "Do you actually want to be a servant forever? I knew after our pack was attacked that I'd never take a mate or have children. You'll be stuck with me until the day you die, unless you call your father. He can revoke the offer. You can return to them and be free of me tonight."

She lifted her chin. "No. I can't do that."

Now he scowled. "Why?"

"I'm not calling my dad to ask him to revoke his offer."

"Are you crazy?"

"No. I'm *desperate*! I already told you why we did this. Nothing has changed. I'm *safe* here. I'd rather be a servant for the rest of my life than let my dad fight in that challenge. It will be to the death! My mom will die with him if he loses. Their bond is too strong for her to survive it breaking."

Frustration filled him, even if Graves could understand the fear of her parents dying. "There are other options. Your father can still step aside but protect you at the same time. Just go live with humans, damn it! Your father can give you that freedom. Alphas have the power to do so."

"No."

"Yes!" he snarled.

"Brandon will come after me if I live with humans. He'll claim I'm a danger to the pack just by knowing they exist. He's that big of a jerk, but in reality, he'll want to come after me purely for revenge, to make me *wish* I was dead. That's practically his ultimate dream come true! I'm not kidding about how much he hates and resents me. Now I've managed to escape, and that's just one more thing he'll want me to pay for. I'm no longer available as a whore for his unmated enforcers. That means he's broken his promise to them. He's going to find me and take me back."

"Then move far away, somewhere he *can't* find you. Easy enough. He'll be too busy learning how to lead your old pack. He can't go trudging around, searching the country for one human. I'll even put the word out to ignore him if he attempts to hire trackers."

"No. I'm not going to live with humans. I might technically be one, but I have nothing in common with them."

He had to work to battle his anger. "You're not staying here."

"You can't make me leave. Dad gifted me to you. So I won't ever be freed, got it, I understand what you're saying. But I'll be protected inside a pack. I'm staying with you."

He snarled. "You're too damn stubborn and making no sense!"

Joni lowered her head and released the couch, crossing her arms over her chest. When she spoke, her voice was resigned. "I'm making perfect sense. You just don't want to hear what I have to say. I'd rather be a servant to a Were than alone in the human world, where I don't belong, without protection. I know you're angry. I'm sorry for that. I'll make it up to you any way I can. You're getting free labor, remember? Just...give it some time." She looked up briefly. "May I return to my room now?"

"No. The kitchen floor needs to be cleaned. Right now." He snapped out the words, pissed beyond reason and feeling petty enough to teach her a lesson. She wanted to be a servant? Fine. He'd treat her like one.

Her body stiffened but without a word, Joni turned, walking into the kitchen. She opened the long cupboard and removed the broom.

With a sigh, he crossed the room, yanked it out of her hand, and shoved it back inside the cupboard.

She kept her head lowered. "It's hard to sweep if you take the broom away. I could use my hands, I guess, but it wouldn't be very effective."

"Do you really think I'm going to make you clean the damn floors right now, in your pajamas?"

"I'm your servant." Her chin lifted, and to his surprise, defiance flared in her brown eyes. "Whether you like it or not."

"You little shit." He reached for her, and she flinched but didn't try to avoid his hand.

He gently gripped her upper arm, careful not to bruise her. "I'm pissed, but I'd never hurt you."

Relief flashed across her face briefly. "That's your call. I'm sorry, Graves, but you're stuck with me. I can't go back."

"You *could* but you *won't*."

She hesitated, then sighed. "I won't." Her gaze studied his. "I'll make this up to you. Somehow, some way. I promise."

He let her go. He'd tried to use logic. Now he'd resort to fear. "I had a true mate who died. Under the very pack law that you're counting on to keep you here, I'm deemed a widower. Do you know what that means for you, Joni?"

She frowned. "No."

He invaded her personal space. "Call your father…or you'll find out."

"I won't do that."

He quickly grabbed her hips, picked her up, and placed her ass on the kitchen island. Fear filled her eyes as he wedged his hips between her parted thighs, her shirt riding up until they were pressed together intimately, and he got right in her face, now they were closer in height.

He inhaled her scent, picking up strawberries from her bathing products, mint from her toothpaste, and pure, warm human female. She smelled nice, and her soft skin felt even better where he clutched her things just above the knee. He hated noticing all that—and even worse, his dick responded. It had been too damn long since he'd gotten laid.

Despite that, Graves didn't attempt to cool his libido. It was better if Joni knew the state he was in. He rocked forward, rubbing his dick against her underwear, letting her feel his growing hard-on. She gasped.

"I can *fuck you*, baby. That's what it means. Do you understand? I can carry your ass upstairs to my bed and bury myself balls deep inside you. No broken laws, since I'm a widower with a human servant. Housework won't be the only thing you're doing around here. Add fucking me whenever the hell I want to your chore list. I'm a Werewolf. I could screw you a dozen times a day." He paused. "Are you ready to call your father *now*?"

He could see that his words shocked her. She'd paled yet again.

"I'm not lying. The law permits me to bed you. Your father unknowingly gave you to a widower. It doesn't matter that I didn't get the chance to claim my mate. No one interprets the ancient laws better than Yasha; she wouldn't say it unless it was true. Now…I'm going to put you down, back away, and you're going make that call to your father. I'll drive you home to your parents tonight. Got it?"

Her hands trembled as she placed them on his chest. "You wouldn't hurt me that way."

His guts twisted when he scented her fear and saw the tears filling her eyes. "Don't manipulate me. You're right. I won't hurt you. But we're done. Find another way to save your own ass."

She took a deep breath and blinked rapidly. "I won't be returned to my pack."

Every muscle in his body turned rigid. "You think I'm bluffing?"

"You don't hurt women."

"You're right. I wouldn't force you—but I *would* seduce you. Do you want blunt? You can screw me over by forcing me to keep you here, but I can fuck you right back." He leaned in closer, slid his hands to her hips, and yanked her even tighter against him. "Literally."

"I don't give you permission."

He snorted. "I don't need it. You're my servant. I can touch you whenever I'd like." To prove his point, he slide his hands under her ass and grabbed both cheeks. He figured groping her ass would do the trick, even as he took care to be gentle with her human body. "Call your daddy."

She held his gaze for a long pause.

"No."

He released her and spun away, wanting to howl in anger and punch something. "Fuck!"

"May I go to bed now?"

He glared at her. "Yes."

She slid off the edge of the island and rushed toward the guest room.

"Wrong direction, Joni."

She froze and glanced over her shoulder, wariness in every line of her worried features. "What do you mean?"

"You're going to be sleeping in my bedroom from now on. Get your ass upstairs. I sleep on the left side of the bed. Oh, and I sleep naked—so you will too."

She fully faced him now. "You can't be serious!"

"I am, servant. Naked. In. My. Bed. Do what you're told."

"You said you wouldn't force me."

"I won't...but I can touch you. I'll do things that will have you *begging* me to fuck you. Think about that, Joni."

She paled yet again.

"If you're determined to stay, it's going to be as hellish for you as it is for me." He forced a cold smile to his lips. "Ready to call your daddy yet, or are you going to climb into my bed as ordered? Your choice."

Her mouth clamped into a tight line. She glared at him, then marched toward the stairs. "I'll rip off your nuts if you try anything."

He jolted at the vicious tone of her threat. It actually impressed him a little. Then it infuriated him. She should be terrified and cowering. "No, you won't. You picked me because I never lose a fight. We both know you wouldn't stand a chance of getting away from me if I decided to pin you down to lick you to within an inch of your life. I'll be up in ten minutes."

Graves fumed after she'd made her way upstairs. He was a fucking idiot! He didn't want her in his bedroom and certainly not naked in his bed. But the alpha challenge took place on Saturday. He only had a few days to make Joni miserable enough to rethink staying with him.

"Damn it," he growled. It was going to be a war of wills—but he planned to win.

He paced the living room. Ten minutes passed quickly, but he wasn't willing to go to bed yet. Part of him hoped she'd defy him, and he'd find her sleeping in the other guest room.

After an hour, he finally crept upstairs.

His bedroom door had been left open and he entered, her scent immediately hitting him. Joni lay huddled in a fetal position on the far right edge of the big mattress, covered up to her head, but her slow breathing assured him she'd fallen asleep.

He moved silently around the bed, spotting her nightshirt, a pair of black panties, and her socks in a neat pile on the floor. She'd stripped.

Shaking his head, he began to remove his own clothing. She was in for a big surprise if she'd thought he was bluffing. He wasn't the type.

Come hell or high water, he never backed down.

Hell came when he climbed into bed, sliding between the sheets with her sleeping just feet away.

Her scent filled his nose, the sound of her breathing slow and steady. He wasn't one to sleep with women, even those he *did* have sex with. All his lovers had been short-term, casual, and they weren't allowed inside his home. It was his private space. And Joni had invaded.

"War," he mouthed, closing his eyes and doing his best to tune her out. He just needed to fall asleep.

Chapter Five

Joni jolted awake when a large hand cupped her ass and squeezed it through the bedding. Her eyes flew open and memory instantly returned.

Graves released her butt, then gave it a light smack. It wasn't enough to hurt, but she jolted again.

"I'm hungry," he rumbled. "Make me breakfast."

She gripped the covers and turned slightly as the bed moved. Graves sat up, using his pillow and the padded dark leather headboard to lean against. The blankets covered his lap but his upper body was completely exposed. She couldn't help but gape a little. He looked muscular wearing his shirt, but it hadn't prepared her for seeing him in the flesh.

So much flesh.

He had tons of muscles and tight abs. Faint scars marred his tan skin. A reminder of what he did for a living. Graves was a Werewolf who'd survived a lot of fights. The scars didn't diminish his appeal. They just added to the enticement.

His hair was mussed, making him look even sexier as she finally glanced up from his stomach and chest. His eyes were narrowed, lips pursed.

"Did you hear me? I'm hungry. You wanted to be a servant. Get your ass out of bed and cook me breakfast."

He was purposely being mean. She nodded. "Fine." She sat up, gripping the covers, then paused. Getting out of bed meant exposing *her* body as well. Every inch would be bared.

"What's the holdup?"

She swallowed. "Can you close your eyes while I get dressed?"

"No. I own you, remember? Don't bother with your nightclothes. Just go downstairs and put on something before you cook. I'd have you do it naked, but I love bacon for breakfast. I'm not cruel enough to risk you getting burned from any grease spatter. I like my bacon crispy but not blackened, by the way."

She hesitated.

"You could give me a blow job instead, if you're determined to stay in bed with me. Your choice."

She twisted her head, shocked at the suggestion. He grinned, a glint in his stormy eyes as he reached down for the blankets covering his lap, as if preparing to expose his cock.

"No!"

He fisted the blankets but didn't shove them down. "Fine. I won't demand that you suck me off. Stay in this bed, though, and I *will* touch you. There's no law against it, after all. *You* could be my breakfast." He slowly ran his tongue over his lips. "One way or another, I'm eating something real soon."

"You're trying to scare me but it's not going to work. I know you won't hurt me. You're too honorable."

His smile faded. "We've already been over this. I won't hurt you, but I'll pin you down and put my mouth on you. I don't bluff, baby. I'm giving you options." He released the blankets with his hand and held up one finger. "Walk out of here naked to go make me breakfast, so I get a good view of you. It's my job to assess people, so I already know you're modest and a bit shy. You're not the type to strut around nude without it embarrassing you."

He held up another finger. "Stay in this bed with me, and find yourself on your back with my face between your thighs. It sure as hell won't hurt. You'll be begging me to fuck you by the time I'm done playing with you. I won't, though, because I don't have condoms. That means your pride will take a hit that'll be tough to recover from."

He put up a third finger. "Agree to call your dad, and I'll close my eyes while you run out of my bedroom. I'll drive you home with both your modesty and pride intact. We can pick up breakfast on the way. No cooking required."

He fisted his hand and dropped it on his lap. "Decide now."

She itched to punch him in his smug-looking face. He was right on all counts. "Please don't be this way, Graves."

A muscle in his jaw twitched but his gaze hardened. "You and your parents forced me to bring you here. I was very clear that I resented it. This is *my* home, and I've been reduced to being *your* caretaker. You think that doesn't piss me off? You know it does. I'm not going to back down. I'll make you miserable until you leave, one way or another. Now—I gave you options. Pick one."

Joni closed her eyes. He had every right to be furious. She'd even expected it. However, none of their careful research had uncovered the fact that he'd met but lost his true mate. She believed him when he said he could touch her now, because he also wasn't known to lie. She'd basically become his sex slave under the old common laws of the packs.

Part of her was extremely grateful that he wasn't a bad person. Someone like Brandon would have done whatever he wanted to her body and not given her *any* options. He'd have enjoyed inflicting pain and humiliation. Graves wouldn't hurt her that way. He was using scare tactics instead.

"I don't want to be your enemy," she whispered, forcing herself to look at him. "But I also can't get my parents killed. My dad will fight Brandon if I go back. I don't think he can win."

He growled and anger glinted in his eyes. "Fine. You can't go back there. I get it. I'll help you obtain a new identity and personally put you on a plane to wherever the hell you want to go. I'll give you ten grand to hold you over until you find a job. Living with humans is better than staying here."

It was a very nice offer; one he didn't have to make. She appreciated that. It was even tempting, after seeing how angry he was to have her in his home. Then she remembered the time she'd spent with humans at school.

The lessons she'd learned the most during her high school years was how much she didn't fit in with those kids, never fully understood them, and how alone she'd felt.

She'd also be at the mercy of human predators without anyone to protect her. The world would swallow her whole, and she doubted she'd survive long. Bad people would target her if they realized she was utterly clueless and all alone. At least here, she'd be surrounded by pack in a world she knew, with rules she understood.

"Can't you just give it a month?" She gave him a pleading look. "I'll stay out of your way by staying in my room when you're home. You'll still get a free cook and housekeeper. I'll help you with your job if I can. I'll learn how to be useful...a receptionist! or I could clean your guns if you teach me how. I know sometimes you have to use them when dealing with certain situations. I'm also good with computers. I'll earn my keep, Graves. It might be a good thing for both of us. We could make this work."

He used both hands to rub his face. A low rumble came from him before he dropped his arms, frowning at her. "It wouldn't work for me."

"You've never tried it before. I'm your first servant," she said, going for humor.

Graves didn't look amused in the least. "I can't have you living here, Joni."

"Why not?"

"It just wouldn't work."

"You don't know that until we give it a shot."

He tilted his head back and closed his eyes. It gave her the opportunity to glance at his chest and stomach again. He really was sexy. That was a problem, but she'd known he was good-looking when they picked him to be her protector. The surprise was how *strongly* she was attracted to him. She'd have to deal with it.

"I can smell you, even if I can't see you." His nostrils flared as he inhaled. Then he lifted his head, his eyes snapping open. "I fuck women and walk away. I don't *live* with them. What do you think is going to happen the next time I come home after a rough job, when my mind is a total mess? It happens from time to time. Should I tell you what that could mean for you?"

She opened her mouth to ask what that had to do with anything, but he cut her off before she could speak.

"I'd probably fuck you to forget whatever nightmare I'd just dealt with. That can't happen for a hundred reasons, but the top of the list is that I can't nail you and then tell you to go home. You'd still be here. In *my* space. And I've never brought women home, ever. Not once. You're the first woman who's slept under the same roof as me that wasn't family. Hell, the first who's slept in a bed with me!

"I don't fuck women in my bed. I never sleep with them. I don't like to talk to them much before, while, or after we screw. And do you know why? *My. Space.* I don't share it with anyone. I don't let anyone get close."

His angry confession surprised her. Joni knew how most unmated Were men behaved. The enforcers who'd guarded her were mostly single, and their homes might as well have had revolving doors, given the traffic from all the different women they were bedding. Males tended to prefer having sex where they felt the most secure. That would be where they slept.

Graves was saying the exact opposite.

"It would get messy between us. This is my peaceful place." He sat up straighter and glared at her. "I'm never taking a mate. I've got a cold, black hole where my heart used to be. I rarely fuck the same woman twice, and those I have don't want anything from me except sex. They get a thrill from being with someone so dangerous. I don't have to give a shit or think about them once they're out of sight."

Joni opened her mouth but he stopped her from talking yet again.

"Did you even happen to notice that I don't have any pets or plants? I'm not cut out for making sure something is fed or taken care of. My phone might ring at any second with news from Arlis that I'm being sent on a job. I'll be gone hours, days, or sometimes even a week or so. You have no friends here. No one to talk to." He paused, taking a deep breath, and his features slightly softened. "I'd have to worry about you. Just…no."

"No one would mess with me. You have a reputation. Everyone fears you."

"What if you fell down the stairs? You're *human*." He shook his head. "What if you get sick? What if I left you my SUV so you could go shopping in one of the human towns, and you were in an accident? Or some asshole human got handsy with you in a parking lot? Don't you get it? I'm responsible for you."

He shook his head again. "I'm not doing this, Joni. I'm not cut out for it. I'm also not risking the day coming when my dick is in charge instead of my brain because I just came back from seeing a murdered child and I'm screwed up inside. I see all kinds of horrible shit in my line of work, and that's another reason why I live alone. I sit in this cabin, by myself, to get my head back together. I don't need the temptation of a woman."

The intimate glimpses into Graves's life had her feeling…sad. No one should have to do what he did for a living, then endure the aftermath alone. She could also tell that he'd given it a lot of thought and consideration. It staggered her a little. He might say he didn't have a heart, but he was wrong. No heartless person considered the impact he might have on those around him after a difficult job, or came up with all those scenarios that could happen to her while he was gone.

"I'm not totally helpless or a klutz, Graves. I've never fallen down the stairs in my life or died from a cold." She paused. "At least if someone were to hurt me here, I know you'd avenge me. No one is going to notice if I die in the human world."

He frowned. "Your parents would."

She shook her head. "My father's brother is completely against the mixing of races. Not just mating and sleeping with them. Fenel doesn't believe Werewolves should interact with humans unless it's unavoidable for business. He considers that a necessary evil. No members of his pack are friends with humans. They don't mingle on a social level. Cell phones are banned, and all calls must go through the pack office land line. That way, Fenel knows what his Weres are up to at all times, especially where the human world is concerned."

"That's barbaric."

"Agreed." She sighed. "My parents getting a call from another pack office wouldn't raise any alarms, but calls coming from *outside* a pack might get them kicked out. Fenel can be paranoid about his pack's safety. My parents omitted the fact that I'm human when they told him they'd adopted an orphan. I can't contact them if I live in the human world. My parents would never know what became of me if you forced me to leave."

Graves scowled. "They could live somewhere else."

"I don't have to tell you that no alpha is going to accept a retired one into their pack unless it's family. My dad never wanted to lead a pack. He got stuck with that job when his alpha was murdered by humans. Dad was a good leader, but his heart was never into it. He always swore he'd step aside if anyone strong enough to hold a pack together challenged him. Now, my parents need to join Fenel's pack. It wouldn't be safe for them to live alone with me. You know that. Don't let your anger cloud your decision."

Graves grimaced. "Your parents would become targets if they lived in the human world."

She nodded. "Especially with my dad's alpha blood. He'd be challenged constantly by rogue Weres the second they got a whiff of him. They can't resist, and I doubt they'd care about fighting fair or taking him on one at a time. Rules of honor don't apply to rogues. That's how lone alphas without a pack are seen. Everyone just seems to want them dead. How they end up alone doesn't matter as long as the threat is eliminated."

Graves gave a grim nod, not arguing because he knew it was true.

"My parents need to live with a pack for protection. It's the kind of community life they're used to. Even if that means I can only call them a few times a year and never see them again, to keep Fenel from finding out I'm human, at least I'll know they're safe and happy. They've wanted this for a long time. My parents finally get to focus all their attention on each other instead of everyone else."

He stared at her for a long time, expression as angry as ever, before gripping the blankets. "I have to piss," he said, swinging his legs off the bed.

Joni closed her eyes. The bed dripped, the covers shifted, and she heard him move across the room on bare feet until a door closed.

She peeked, making sure he'd really entered his bathroom. He had. She shoved off the covers and quickly put on her nightshirt and undies.

Graves came out wearing a towel wrapped around his waist a few minutes later. He dried his washed hands by wiping them along the sides of his hips. Their gazes met, and he frowned. "I'm sorry for the position you've found yourself in, Joni. But you can't stay with me. I'll give you my cell phone number and buy you a plane ticket to take you far out of Brandon's reach. Think of someplace you want to go. We'll hit the bank on the way to the airport for the ten grand I promised. I can also get you a new identity, so trackers won't be able to find you if that asshole hires some."

She opened her mouth to protest.

He cut her off before she could speak. "I give my word that I'll come help you if you're ever in trouble. That's the best I can do. You're not staying here. Now get out of my bedroom and go get dressed in travel clothes. We leave in ten minutes."

"Graves—"

"No." His voice deepened and his eyes seemed to harden, giving her a cold stare. "Option time is over. This is the way it's going to be."

"Please!"

He looked furious. "The only other choice is sending you to the VampLycans in Alaska. They'd take you in and keep you safe."

"We heard your pack was associated with them. I'm not comfortable with that."

"You haven't even met one, have you? I know plenty of them. Hell, I'm related by blood to one of the clans. VampLycans are highly honorable, and they'd never hurt a woman or force you to do shit. You'd be in good hands with my cousin's clan."

"No," she said. "I'm staying with you and your pack."

"I'll knock your ass out, dress you myself, and you'll wake up at the goddamn airport, if that's what it takes. As a matter of fact, the more I think about it, the better the VampLycans sound. I'll call my cousin to meet your plane in Anchorage. Now, are you going to dress yourself, or should I do it?" He took a threatening step closer.

He meant it. Joni could hear it in his voice and see the determination in his chilly glare. It was as if he'd turned off every emotion but anger.

With no options left, she fled his bedroom.

Graves gritted his teeth and let Joni run down the stairs. A door slammed seconds later. He returned to the bathroom, dropped the towel, and turned on the shower. He hated to be a dick, but he couldn't allow her to stay. A human wasn't his problem or his responsibility. Hell, he was doing more than most people would to help her, after the way she'd been forced into his life.

He dressed in faded jeans, a black heavy metal band T-shirt, and donned running shoes. He put his watch on last, before shoving his wallet into his back pocket from his nightstand. His list of to-dos streamed through his mind.

Breakfast. Bank. Call Wen to meet her in Alaska. Airport. In that order. Then he'd be rid of Joni for good.

He'd still give her money. It would be shitty to dump Joni on Trayis's clan flat broke. She'd need lots of winter gear. Alaska got damn cold. Wen could help her buy whatever she needed when she arrived. His cousin owed him a few favors. He knew he'd keep Joni safe.

A little guilt surfaced at passing that particular torch, but better the clan than him. He had too much on his plate already. He started walking out of his bedroom but then remembered his cell on his nightstand. Just as he reached for it, the screen lit up, showing his alpha's name. He lifted it, taking the call.

"What's up, Arlis?"

"I know the timing is shit, considering what you're dealing with, but I need you to come to the office ASAP."

"What's up?"

"Elmer Gillards called the pack line. He's demanding to speak with you. I didn't think you would appreciate me giving him your direct number. The guy is a total dickweed."

"Why didn't you just hang up on him?"

"Official annoying protocol that I need to follow. I already clued him in that Jerry was found guilty of being a mate abuser who murdered a pack mate with a gun instead of having the guts to fight fair, but Elmer's going the formal route. He demanded a verbal report directly from you on why you put down one of his. At first he demanded that you come into his territory to tell him in person. We've negotiated to a phone call after I mentioned he'd have to pay a huge fee if you had to travel. Your time is expensive." Arlis chuckled. "I might have tripled the price I normally quote. I knew you'd probably have to kill him if you went there, and we don't need that shitshow. Get over here now."

"He's just doing this to save face with his pack."

"Yeah." Arlis snorted. "By being a whiny pain in my ass."

"I'm on my way." Graves disconnected the call and went downstairs. "Joni? Get out here."

She opened the bedroom door wearing black pants and a baggy blue shirt. He flinched inwardly when he noticed her red, swollen eyes. He'd made her cry. *Fuck!*

"My alpha called. I've got to go to the office. This doesn't change a damn thing but the timing, and I shouldn't be gone long. Be ready to go when I get back."

He quickly turned away, not wanting to see if his harsh words would make her start crying all over again. Guilt had him stomping toward the door.

"Do you want breakfast before you go?"

"No time." He opened the front door and closed it behind him, taking a path through the woods. Fresh air would clear his head and cool his temper.

He reached the pack office and nodded hello to Darlene. She was Arlis's secretary. She motioned for him to go into the alpha's office. As he passed her, she reached out, brushing her fingers over his arm. He stopped, staring at her as she remained seated behind the desk.

"You look stressed. I heard about the servant-nightmare situation." Her fingers caressed his arm again.

He pulled away from her touch.

"I can help you with that. The one time you came to my house was fun. I'm not looking for anything but a good hard fuck. I haven't had the greatest week either. We could release some aggression together."

"Thanks for the offer, but no. Shit's complicated right now." Graves continued into the private office, happy to dodge that bullet. He wasn't lying to Joni; he almost never slept with the same woman twice.

Besides, he'd slept beside her in his bed. She'd been feet away from him all night, and he'd inhaled her scent with every breath. It seemed...wrong to touch another woman right now, with the memory of Joni still so strong in his head.

Arlis sat behind his desk, reading a file. "Incident report from Martin. Last night, two pups snuck out to go swimming in the river."

He took a seat across from his alpha. "Are they okay?"

"Both are good swimmers. They just frightened their parents when they noticed they were gone." He picked up a pen, writing on the top of the folder. "One week of picking up trash along the banks. That should teach them to stay in bed and cure their eagerness to play in water for a while." He leaned back after dropping the folder and putting the pen down. "I spoke to Yasha first thing this morning. Do you want to explain what's up with the strange way you reacted to what she had to say?" Arlis asked, giving him an obvious sniff.

"I didn't fuck Joni, if that's what you're sniffing for. I thought about using it to scare her into wanting to go home. Told her I could fuck her anytime I wanted since I'm technically a widower, a little fact she and her father obviously didn't know."

"I see. So she's going back to her pack?"

He slouched in the chair. "No. She's a tough little shit for being a human. Stubborn."

A grin split Arlis's face.

"Fuck you. No offense."

"I'm not amused for the reason you might think. I just can't see a woman standing her ground when you, of all people, are purposely attempting to make one flee. Hell, some of my enforcers would retreat from you, Graves."

"I'm here to call Elmer. Not to have you bust my balls."

"Let the whiner wait. It's not like he doesn't know why his men keep getting into trouble, or can be surprised that you judged death. How many of his previous pack does this make that you've had to put down?"

"Just over half a dozen."

"Yeah. That prick knows why they keep ending up dead." Arlis paused. "Talk to me, Graves."

He adjusted his ass, uncomfortable in the hard seat. "There's not much to say. Joni thinks she's saving her parents by living with me. I get that, but I can't let her stay. This doesn't work for me. End of story. I told her I'd take her to the airport, give her ten grand so she has money of her own, and I'll send her ass to the VampLycans. I'm sure Trayis will accept her. Wen can pick her up in Anchorage and take her back to the clan."

Arlis's features twisted with disapproval.

"What?" He hated that look on his alpha's face. "Do you think Trayis will say no?"

"That's not it. You know that Mandy is going to be deeply disappointed, right?"

Graves inwardly cringed. His mother would lose her shit. Probably yell at him. Worse, if it upset her enough, she'd cry. Then he'd feel guilty. And any tears would also really piss off his father and younger brother.

"Mandy already called Yasha to see if there's any way for her to adopt the human as a daughter, instead of her being a servant. Your mother is heavily invested in this Joni and she hasn't even been here a full day. Sending her away isn't going to go over well."

"I don't want Joni living with me." Graves slid his ass in the seat again, full-on fidgeting now.

"Does she cry a lot?"

Not until this morning. Graves didn't mention that, though. "No."

"Tell me more about her."

Graves carefully studied his alpha. "Why? Are you thinking about accepting her into the pack?" He felt a surge of hope at the thought. If she was accepted as pack, his mother could take her in, make sure she was well protected. He didn't care *where* Joni lived, as long as it wasn't in his cabin.

But that hope was dashed when Arlis snorted. "Not if I want to keep my job without having to kill some idiots after they question my judgement." He shook his head. "I'd get challenged by at least a few of them until everyone gets to know Joni and has a feel for what kind of person she is. No one is just going to blindly accept her as a member of our pack. It's going to take time. What does your gut say about her? Be honest."

"Rogues killed her family when she was five, but she feels no hatred for Werewolves. Pack seems to make her feel safe, and the idea of not living with one scares her." He felt like shit for admitting that to his alpha, considering he planned to send her to live with the VampLycans. They were good, honorable people, but clans weren't run the same way as a pack. It would probably be a hard adjustment for her.

"Joni is highly protective of Alpha Pete and his mate. He's been challenged by an asshole who hates Joni. She thinks Alpha Pete will die if he's forced to fight to keep her safe. He plans to step aside, by the way, now that she's no longer with his pack. But not even me being a dick to her last night made her willing to go home if it meant risking his life. She knows her mom won't survive the mate bond breaking if her father dies."

Arlis reached up and rubbed his temple. "How exactly were you being a dick to her?"

"I implied that I'd fuck her if she didn't call her father and agree to go home. I figured she'd freak. She's not exactly a robust human. She flat-out refused to take that exit option. Joni is determined to stay, regardless of me threatening to seduce her."

"She *must* be desperate."

Graves frowned. "Thanks a lot."

Arlis had the nerve to laugh. "I didn't mean it that way. You scare people and you damn well know it. I can't picture an average human not running away screaming if you threatened to get naked when you're in a bad mood. That's all. You'd think she'd be especially terrified, considering she met you after you just sentenced someone to death."

"You'd think." Graves straightened in the chair and gripped the arms, dropping his gaze.

"Why do you look perplexed?"

He refused to look at his alpha. "She sees my job as something to respect. It's fucking weird."

Silence stretched between them, and Graves felt watched. He finally met Arlis's gaze. His alpha had an odd look on his face.

"What?"

"She's not afraid of you or what you do? Is that what you're saying?"

"Joni said her and her parents did their research on me, whatever the hell that means, and she feels certain I won't hurt her."

"I like her already." Arlis sucked in a deep breath and blew it out. "You're going to hate me, because I hardly ever pull my alpha weight with you. This time I am—and you *will* obey me. I forbid you from handing off this Joni to anyone else. She's to remain in your house."

"No." Graves shook his head.

"Yes. Give it some time."

He was furious. "For what?"

"We all worry about you, Graves. You're a part of this pack but you keep everyone at arm's length emotionally. I can't tell you how many times your mother has sat in that chair, pleading with me to stop sending you on jobs because she's worried all those kills are going to eventually push you over the edge. Every year you grow colder and more distant.

And trust me, I understand. I deeply appreciate what you do and respect the hell out of you. I know you aren't going to snap. I have absolute faith in your inner strength."

Graves stared into Arlis's eyes, seeing only sincerity there. His alpha's words deeply touched him and that calmed his temper a bit.

"But it also makes some of the pack anxious, because they think you might lose it one day. I think they would've been happy if you'd adopted a fucking puppy, just to show everyone that you could care about something, *anything*, but instead you were handed a human. That could turn into a great thing, even if you don't see it. Do you understand what I'm saying?"

"No. I love my brother and parents. Anyone who thinks I'm not capable of having feelings are fucking morons. Tell *that* to anyone who's worried about me snapping."

"Your family is different. I'm just being honest with you, Graves. *I* know you have a heart. And I realize that you never plan on taking a mate, because it's not fair to ask someone to settle without the kind of bonds a true mate creates. But life literally just handed you a woman, Graves. One who needs you. She's a human with no expectations about having a true mate. Need I say more? Because I will—she's also not afraid of you. Keep her. She's a goddamn miracle that fell into your lap. Have the smarts to see her for the opportunity that she represents."

Graves sat there stunned, his anger building.

Arlis sighed, sensing his fury. "Or not. Either way, she stays until the pack can accept her. Rogues killed her family. She's a human raised by our kind. I'll accept her as soon as I'm able to do so without anyone raising hell about adding an unknown single female into the pack. Until then, you were right—tag, you're it."

Graves was stuck with Joni. "I don't fucking deserve this."

"You *deserve* happiness. Whether living with her is miserable or not, that's up to you. It's your choice. Now, let's place this call to Elmer and deal with his whiny ass." Arlis reached for his phone. "We're done with personal shit. Let's get down to business."

* * * * *

Joni stood when Graves stormed into the cabin and flinched when he slammed the front door closed. He looked enraged. Every muscle in her body seemed to tense when his stormy gaze landed on her and he halted in his tracks. A vicious snarl tore from him.

"You get to stay. Not my choice. Unpack your shit."

The news stunned her.

"My alpha insisted." He fisted his hands at his sides. "This is utter bullshit!"

She should have felt some guilt but relief flooded her instead. She'd spent the last hour since he'd left feeling sick to her stomach with worry about what she'd face living with the VampLycans. The unknown terrified her. "We'll make this work."

That was the wrong thing to say. Graves snarled again and she saw some fur sprout along his exposed arms and the back of his fisted hands. He spun away, pacing and refusing to look in her direction.

Joni was tempted to creep away from him slowly, since he was in such a bad mood, but she didn't. Her job was to take care of him, whether he liked it or not. "Are you hungry? I can make you something."

His head snapped her way. "Go to your room. Just stay out of my way until I calm down."

"Okay." She fled into the downstairs bedroom, softly closing the door.

She heard Graves growling and something thumped loudly, as if he'd punched a wall or maybe kicked a piece of furniture. More guilt piled up over his apparent upset, but at least she got to stay. Joni would have been miserable if he'd forced her to leave. Instead, it seemed Graves would be the one to suffer.

Why can't he compromise? He gets a free housekeeper and cook out of the deal. She could see it would be a pain for him to have someone sharing his home, but she meant it when she said she would stay out of his way.

Joni took a seat on the bed, listening to him snarl again from the other room. At one point he stomped up the stairs, then came back down within minutes.

"I have a job," he yelled. "I'll be gone a few days. Get out here."

She stood and opened the bedroom door. Graves held a backpack in his fist, his anger displayed on his face as he glared at her.

"Don't leave the cabin or answer my land line. No, wait. Answer the phone. That way I can check on you."

"I have a cell phone. Do you want the number?"

Graves hesitated, then slung the backpack over his shoulder, withdrawing his cell from his pocket. He tapped the screen. "Give it to me."

She rattled off her number.

"Answer me when I call. Got it?"

"Yes. Is there anything I can do?"

He growled. "No. Just stay inside, don't answer the land line phone, and stay away from the damn stairs. My bedroom is back to being off limits. I'm out of here."

She watched him storm toward the door. "Be safe and um...good luck."

He yanked open the front door. "Lock this behind me and keep it that way. I'll be back in a few days. Don't get sick. That's an order."

Joni flinched when the door slammed, but she went to the door and obediently twisted the bolt. A minute later, she heard the engine of his SUV roar to life and he took off, gravel spinning beneath his wheels.

"I get to stay." She turned to stare at his home and sighed.

Chapter Six

Joni folded a towel and piled it on the dryer before reaching for another one inside the machine.

"Hello."

The unexpected male voice had her gasping and spinning around. Fear swamped her when she stared up at the big man filling the doorway to the laundry room. He smiled and lifted both hands, palms out in a calming gesture. His black hair was cut short, and he stared back at her with blue eyes in a tan, handsome face.

"I didn't mean to startle you. Sorry. You must not have heard me knocking with the washer going. I'm Micah. Graves is my older brother. I have a house key, and my brother asked me to bring you some groceries. I put them on the island in the kitchen."

Her hammering heart slowed as she recovered from being startled. "Hi."

"You're Joni." His gaze slowly lowered down her body before he flat-out grinned. "You're a tiny thing. It's been killing our mom that Graves has forbidden her from coming to see you. Our dad has had to prevent her from sneaking over here at least a dozen times. Feel sorry for the poor bastard, because Mom is a handful. She's going to love you. Mom is pint-sized too."

Joni wasn't sure how to respond to any of that. She wasn't exactly tiny for a human, but then again, she wasn't as big as most Werewolf women.

"It's kind of funny when you see my parents together, actually. Dad..." He lifted one hand up, to just over the top of his head. "Mom..." He put his other hand mid-chest. "She's a runt, but never underestimate her. She's got more energy than five women combined and is not someone you want to piss off. She turns meaner than shit when riled. When her and my father first started feeling out if they were mates, some other bitches hit on him, thinking she couldn't do anything about it. Mom kicked their asses." He dropped his hands to his sides. "You still look a little spooked. Don't be. I'm harmless."

Not so much spooked as surprised. She'd never met a more chatty Were. He was the polar opposite of Graves. "I'm glad to hear that. It's nice to meet you. You said you brought groceries? Thank you."

"No problem." Micah backed up, grinning again. "I don't want you to feel trapped. Come out to the kitchen, I swear I don't bite. Graves said you were raised with a pack?"

She followed him into the kitchen, staying several feet behind. "Yes."

"Excellent. Then you know you're under the protection of my brother and no one would dare hurt you. Again, I'm sorry for startling you. I *did* pound on the door. I actually got worried when you didn't answer. I'm glad you're okay." He glanced around. "Damn. This place has never been cleaner. You've been busy the past two days while my brother's been gone."

She simply nodded.

He rounded the island to put it between them and pointed at the bags. "Eggs, milk, various meats, and I bought you a chocolate cake. I just basically grabbed whatever I thought you'd eat. Mom gave me a list too.

That bag is by the front door." He winked. "Girl stuff. I'm cool with buying pads and shit. Mom thought you might need them, and some other intimate things. Razors, shampoo and conditioner. Deodorant. I hope it's all brands you like. Mom and I tried to call before I went shopping but you didn't answer."

"Graves told me not to answer his phone."

Micah sighed and looked irritated. "My big brother can be an ass."

"I understand why he doesn't want me taking calls."

He cocked his head slightly, staring at her.

"Graves is unmated. Women might get the wrong impression if another female answered his phone."

He grinned. "Ah. I don't think women call Graves. Hell, I don't even think he gives his numbers to any. Home or cell. It's not like he regularly sees anyone." He looked around again. "How are you doing with him gone?"

"Great."

"Not bored shitless? Going stir crazy?"

"No."

"You've been cooped up inside for two days, all alone. I'd be going bat-shit nuts."

She smiled slightly. "I'm used to staying inside a lot."

"That's pretty sad. Why?"

Micah seemed friendly enough, but she felt leery about sharing too many personal details about her life with a stranger. He certainly wasn't standoffish, like most of the Werewolves she knew, but most of the ones she'd spent time with were enforcers. Joni was curious about his position in the pack was but refused to be nosey. They hadn't researched Graves's family beyond knowing he was close to them.

But Micah clearly expected an answer. He gazed at her expectantly, waiting.

"I worked in the pack house. Once a week I'd go shopping for groceries and basic supplies, but I'm used to staying inside more often than not. I cooked for the unmated enforcers and the elderly in my old pack three times a day."

That answer didn't seem to sit well with him, given his scowl. "I thought you were adopted into your pack. Treated like a daughter, not a servant. At least until you were gifted to Graves."

"I *am* adopted. I'm also an unmated female. I was given an indoor job that kept me safe."

"From what?"

"Do you mind if I put the groceries away?"

"Go ahead." Micah moved out of the kitchen but hovered at the edge of the living room.

She began to empty the bags onto the island and opened the fridge.

"Safe from what? You didn't answer," he reminded Joni.

"I'm human. My parents worried about me, more so than other unmated females. I don't have claws to defend myself or the strength Werewolves do. A few of the pack didn't respect me because of that. It wasn't many, but it only takes one to hurt me, right?" She glanced at

Micah to see his reaction—and regretted it. Anger crinkled his mouth and eyes.

It was time to change the subject and ask the question she really wanted the answer to most. "Anyway...my dad only allowed his enforcers to be alone with me. They gave their oath to keep me safe. Is Graves coming home today?"

"It depends on how long it takes to..." He went quiet. "Never mind."

She frowned. "Judge someone? Find someone? I know what Graves does for a living."

Micah studied her with narrowed eyes. "Do you?"

"He's a judge. And an executioner, when the crime is bad enough. I know he tracks down killers too."

"Doesn't that frighten you?"

"Worried, is more the term I'd use. Graves could get hurt."

"I mean, doesn't it frighten you to live with him?"

"No. Why should it?"

"Because he kills people."

"Bad people."

"That doesn't scare you? Make you leery of him?"

"Again...why should it?" She felt confused.

"Again...he *kills* people."

"I heard you the first time. I'm aware. And like I said, *bad* people. Murderers. Abusers. Probably rapists. Total scum. He's doing a great service to packs *and* humans. Do *you* have a problem with what your brother does? Graves is a hero, Micah. You should understand that."

Micah just gawked at her.

"What?" She scowled. "Graves *is* a hero. Every killer he puts down means fewer lives that are taken. He gives the families of their victims peace of mind, knowing their loved ones have been avenged. It takes bravery and courage to go after dangerous people that most others would run away from."

"Goddamn." Micah grinned suddenly. "I think I love you."

It was her turn to gawk at him. She also backed up and firmly put the island between them.

He laughed. "Not in the 'I want to fuck and keep you' way. I just mean, besides our alpha, a few of our pack members, and our family, most people fear my brother or at least give him a wide berth. I love your *attitude*. Is that better? No need to run from me and lock yourself in a room."

She relaxed. "Everyone should appreciate what Graves does."

"Oh man, he has *got* to keep you." Micah grinned again. "Please say yes if he asks you to be his mate."

Graves brother had a way of shocking the hell out of her. The siblings really were nothing alike except for a physical resemblance, which she was finally noticing. "You've got it all wrong. Your brother is definitely not interested in me that way."

"He should be. Graves is super-smart about most things but dumb as a post when it comes to women. You need to seduce him into mating you."

She gasped. "Are you crazy?"

"No. Why would you ask?"

"Your brother isn't the type to settle down. Especially with someone like me."

"You mean someone who's smart, cute as hell, and isn't afraid of him?" Micah winked. "Seduce him into claiming you, Joni." His expression grew serious. "Alpha Arlis would be cool with it. We're a progressive pack. No old-school bullshit with rules of only mating to our own kind. Hell, I could bring a Vamp home and my alpha would let me keep her. Not that I would. I'm a day person. It would be hell, mating with someone who's killed by sunshine. Total deal-breaker for me."

Joni shook her head, still stunned at the things he was saying. "I'm certain your parents wouldn't approve."

"Of a Vamp? Probably not, since a Vampire woman couldn't get pregnant. My mom would be heartbroken. She's been all over my ass to give her grandkids. But our parents would totally be cool with it if Graves mated *you*. Dad and Mom would just love the fact that my brother found someone. You being human isn't an issue. I bet my mom would even stop throwing unmated women at me for a while if Graves knocked you up." His gaze lowered to her stomach, and he sniffed loudly. "Are you on anything to prevent pregnancy?"

She leaned against the island to hide her stomach from view. "You *are* crazy, aren't you?"

He chuckled. "Maybe, but I'm harmless. Are you on birth control?"

"That's none of your business."

"I like that you're not submissive enough to answer me. Graves needs someone who challenges him. Stand up to him, Joni. He'd never hurt you, even when you start pitching shit at his thick skull to knock some sense into him."

"I would never."

"Give it time. You will once you get to know my brother better."

"I'm a servant who knows her place."

"Listen, that title is only being used to keep you safe inside our pack from whatever you needed a protector for. No one else keeps servants here. You want to stay with him? Be what Graves *actually* needs. You were raised with a pack, so you should be versed in matings. There's no bitch who'll come along and lure him away, since his true mate died before he could claim her. He protects everyone, but he needs a lover and a partner. Someone who's there for *him*. Maybe think about becoming that person, since you're here."

He reached into his back pocket and withdrew a card. He placed it on the other side of the island, his expression sober. "My phone number. Graves was sent to track a killer of homeless humans, about sixty miles from here. Four deaths have been reported so far. The human police think it's a serial killer, but a Werewolf from another pack works at the morgue. She said the bodies reek of Vampire. That's why Graves got called in. He's the best tracker there is. He almost caught the bastard last night, but the Vamp hurt a human to get away. Graves had to let him flee while he give medical aid to the injured teenager. He'll find the Vamp soon, though. My brother's *that* good. In the meantime, call me if you need anything."

Micah took a few steps toward the front door before looking back at her. "Oh, and don't be frightened if you happen to see a small blonde woman breaking into the cabin. That'll be my mom. Her name is Mandy.

At some point, she's going to be able to fool my dad and sneak over here. She's *really* excited to meet you. Mom always wanted a daughter, and you're now the closest thing she's ever had." He winked yet again, then headed for the front door.

Joni watched Micah leave, her mind stuck on the things he'd said about mating. He was right; she *was* versed on the subject. And unlike what her dad had thought, Graves would never feel an overwhelming desire to leave her for another woman, since his own true mate had died. Though, he still might prefer his own kind.

She walked over to the couch and sat down, pulling her legs up and getting comfortable.

She *could* become Grave's mate...if he was willing to form that bond with her. Werewolves called it settling when they committed to someone who wasn't their true mate. It wasn't an ideal situation for their kind, but the thought of being able to keep Graves forever appealed to her. He was the kind of man she'd never dared to hope for.

The real hurdle would be getting him on board with that idea. He was probably attracted to strong fighter types. And of course, women who actually enjoyed sex. Neither described her. Though, sometimes alpha types mated to more submissive females. But it didn't happen often.

She closed her eyes and sighed. "Well, nothing good ever comes easy. I've got to really work for it. I just need to figure out how to appeal to him."

* * * * *

Graves entered his home, trying to be quiet. It was past two in the morning. He locked the door and cocked his head, listening. He didn't hear Joni at all, not even her breathing. He sat his backpack down by the door and strode over to the guest room.

The door stood open and the perfectly made bed was empty.

He tensed. Had she left? Changed her mind about returning home to her parents? Her scent lingered, though. It wasn't faded as if she'd been gone for long.

He rushed up the stairs to check the other guest room. The idea of her being gone should have thrilled him, but instead he was filled with worry—until he picked up the faint sounds of slow, even breathing.

He halted at his open bedroom door, staring at the small form sleeping on the right side of his bed.

He inhaled Joni's scent. *What in the hell is she doing?* He wasn't angry, despite ordering her to stay out of his room. He felt more confused than anything. He crept closer, his eyes adjusting to the darkness.

She lay on her side facing him and the covers were down enough to reveal her bare shoulders and the top of her chest, some cleavage showing. His dick hardened at the sight, realizing she was nude.

"What in the hell?"

She jolted awake with a gasp and clutched at the bedding, sitting up. "Graves?"

"Who else? What are you doing in my bed?"

She turned her head, and he followed her gaze to his nightstand clock.

"It's after two." She looked in his direction. "Did you find the killer Vampire and take him out?"

She surprised him again. "How did you know about that?"

"Micah told me when he dropped off the groceries."

"I took care of that problem."

"Are you hungry? I could make you something."

"I grabbed some burgers from a drive-thru on my way home." He scowled. "What are you doing in my bed? Answer me."

"Can we turn on a light? I can't see you. You're just a dark shadow."

"I need a shower. I have Vampire blood on me."

"Okay."

He opened his mouth but then closed it on a swallow. "I'll be back."

He hurried into the bathroom, shut the door, and didn't bother with the lights as he began to strip. He went to throw his clothes into the hamper, but stopped. It wasn't full anymore. Joni must have done his laundry, even though he'd told her not to.

He growled as he got into the shower and turned on the water, scrubbing every inch of his body with cold water to cool down. It seemed Joni purposely wanted to infuriate him. She'd entered his bedroom. Taken away his dirty clothes. Was naked in his bed.

Suspicion filled his thoughts, and he growled again.

He finished his shower and dried off, wrapping the towel around his waist as he jerked open the bathroom door. The nightstand lamp nearest her had been turned on, and she remained in his bed. His gaze lowered to

Joni's bared skin, just above where she clutched the blanket to hide her breasts.

"Fucking Micah. Did he tell you I wanted you waiting for me in my bed, without your clothes on?"

"No."

He saw heat flush her cheeks. Her chin tucked down, and Joni seemed to stare at the floor between them.

"Then why did you breach my bedroom? Touch my dirty clothes? Climb into my bed?"

She lifted her chin, and her gaze finally locked with his. "I'm not returning to my old pack. You implied what the cost would be. So...here I am."

His jaw dropped. Irritation swiftly followed as he clenched his teeth together again. "Get out of my room, now."

She lowered her chin to stare at the floor again. "No."

"What did you say?"

"No."

He could smell a faint tinge of fear coming off her as she defied him. "You'll do as I tell you. Get out of my bed, leave my room, and get your ass back to your own. *Now.*" He snarled the last word.

The scent of her fear grew stronger as she threw back the covers, slid out of bed, and quickly walked bare-ass naked around the bed and out of his room.

He took in every inch of her—and hated the way his body responded. He closed his eyes, listening to Joni's ragged breathing as she hurried down the stairs before a door closed below.

He sighed, took deep breaths, and reminded himself that it had just been too long since he'd gotten laid, considering how tempted he was to go after Joni. It couldn't happen though.

His brother was somehow behind Joni's unruly behavior. Micah loved to pull pranks.

He walked over to his bedroom door and closed it, leaning against the door. Graves stared down at his stiff dick, lifting part of the damp towel and snarling again. "Not fucking funny, bro."

He shoved away from the door and dropped the towel, throwing his body onto the bed. He lay on his back, his dick still hard, and turned his head to glare at the light. He rolled toward the lamp, finding the bed still warm where Joni had slept as he reached to turn it off. He wiggled around, shoved at the covers, and slid his body under the sheets.

A fainter scent filled his nose, something besides her fear.

He pushed down the sheets and sniffed where Joni had lain. He knew two things instantly.

She'd been aroused while in his bed…and she was ovulating.

He bolted upright, breathing hard. Had she come to him because she was in the equivalent of human heat? Did she *need* him?

He was off the bed before he made the decision to get up and halfway to the door before he froze.

"No way," he rasped. He turned on his heel and entered his bathroom, turned the shower back on, and reached for the body wash. He'd jack off before he risked getting her pregnant by accident. He didn't need that complication.

Chapter Seven

Joni ended the call with her father. As planned, he'd stepped aside when challenged and Brandon had allowed her parents to immediately leave the territory without a fight. Her parents were currently on their way to live with the uncle she'd never be allowed to meet. They swore to call her again when they arrived in Fenel's territory, before their cell phones were destroyed.

She got up and walked into the kitchen, staring out the window over the sink. Tears blinded her. It was tough enough being away from her mother and father. They had always been a close-knit family. It made her sad to know she would never hug them again. A few phone calls a year was the best she could hope for.

Her thoughts switched to the house she'd once called a home. That was lost to her forever, too. It would now belong to the new alpha. It saddened her but at the same time, she was relieved there hadn't been a fight to the death. Part of her had worried that Brandon would be so enraged over her disappearance that he'd force the fight. Thankfully, he'd proven himself smarter than she'd thought. The pack would never have forgiven him for killing their beloved alpha when it wasn't necessary.

Still, a shiver of dread ran down her spine as she thought about Brandon now being the alpha of her old pack. He would soon learn that her father had left him a few unpleasant surprises. Her dad had done it for the good of the pack. Not just to be petty.

Her nemesis likely wouldn't see it that way. He'd want revenge.

Deep down, she knew Brandon was probably already thinking up ways to get his claws into her. She wouldn't put it past him to make a formal request for her return. The jerk wasn't the sort to ever let go of a grudge. He'd love to see her degraded until her spirit was utterly broken.

Would Graves send her back to her old pack if Brandon asked? Her new owner had made it clear that he didn't want her in his home or under his protection. Handing her over to her old pack would be the easiest way to be rid of her for good. She doubted she'd survive a week with Brandon and his new enforcers before she wished for death.

Fear had her wiping her tears hastily and leaning heavily against the counter. She was just glad no one was witnessing her small breakdown. The morning after Graves had found her in his bed, he was gone before she woke. He hadn't left a note. She had no idea where he was or when he'd be back. Two days had already passed.

She pushed away from the sink and opened the fridge. There was still plenty of food. Her appetite had been lacking since her sad attempt at seduction. Joni studied the contents but nothing looked good. She closed the fridge and took a seat on the couch.

Living in a pack, Joni had often witnessed how aggressive women could be with men they wanted to bed. They tended to walk right up to Werewolves, press their bodies against them, even outright grope their cocks to get the guys hot and bothered. She wasn't a Were though, nor was she aggressive. She'd hoped Graves would take her simply because she was naked in his bed, offering herself.

"I was wrong," she muttered.

The sound of an engine had her getting up and peeking out the front window by the door. Graves parked his SUV in his usual spot and climbed out of the driver's side.

She backed away and felt a bit panicked. *Should I hide? Retake my seat on the couch? Perhaps rush into the kitchen to try to look busy?* She couldn't make up her mind.

Graves unlocked the front door and opened it. Their gazes met, and he instantly frowned. He stepped inside, closed the door, and dropped his black backpack on the floor.

"Hello." Joni lowered her gaze.

"You said you would stay out of my way when I'm home. Do that now."

His gruff tone and words were a verbal slap. She swallowed hard and backed up. "I'm sorry." She hurried toward the downstairs guest room but paused before entering. "My father stepped down as alpha today. Brandon didn't demand a fight. My parents safely made it out of the territory."

"That's good news."

She kept her back to him. "Can we talk?"

"No."

Tears filled her eyes again. "I just have one thing to say. Please? It's important."

"I don't want to talk about the other night."

She was actually relieved; that wasn't the topic on her mind at the moment. "Brandon will probably give you and your alpha the option to return me. Please don't send me back. I beg you." She dared turn her head, staring at him. "I know you're angry because you don't want me here, but have mercy, please. Brandon and his unmated enforcers won't."

She walked into the bedroom, softly closing the door behind her. Long minutes passed as she splashed water on her face in the bathroom to wash away her tears, using a soft towel to pat her face dry.

"Joni? Come here."

She hesitated at the harsh order bellowed through the door, then straightened her shoulders and returned to the living room. Graves stood holding a beer in the kitchen, glaring at her from where he leaned against the island. She lowered her gaze and folded her hands together over her stomach to be the picture of meek.

"I would *never* hand you over to that asshole or his friends. You told me what he's like and what they'd do to you. I might be pissed, but I'm not a cold-hearted bastard."

"Thank you," she whispered.

"I can't stand the scent of fear. I could smell yours the moment I stepped in the door. Enough of that shit. Got it?"

She nodded.

"I might not like being forced to be your protector but that doesn't mean I'd sacrifice your life to get out from under this. Am I clear?"

"Yes. Thank you."

"Stop being so damn grateful," he snarled. "It's getting on my nerves."

"Sorry."

He sighed. "Are you afraid of me, or is the fear because you thought I'd hand you over to your pack's new alpha?"

"I'm afraid of Brandon and his enforcers."

"Look at me."

She lifted her gaze to his. He still glared at her.

"Why the hell were you in my bed the other night when I got home? I know my brother had something to do with that. I'm right, aren't I?"

A blush crept into her cheeks, making her face feel hot. "I thought you didn't want to talk about it."

"Answer the damn question."

Joni jerked at his snarled words. "I want to stay with you." That was honest enough without her having to admit she'd hoped he'd claim her.

"Damn." Graves spun around, took a long swig of his beer, and slammed the bottle on the island. He kept his back to her. "Don't do it again." He turned slowly, giving her a look. "You were ovulating. Do you understand what that means? I get that you probably can't tell, but I picked up the scent on my sheets."

She should just say yes and flee to her room. Instead, she stiffened her spine and drew in a deep breath to steady her nerves. "My pack healer had a talk with me when I hit maturity, assuming I'd become sexually active. We discussed the issues that I would face. You can take me to a human doctor to get me implanted with an IUD, even double it up with birth control pills. Between both of those, the healer said there would be zero chance of an accidental pregnancy occurring with a Werewolf."

His eyes widened but he said nothing, just reached for his beer, taking another swig. He held it so tight she worried that he'd break the glass.

"I thought about going to see a human doctor myself at the time, but my parents would have flipped out. I wasn't allowed to go anywhere without an enforcer because they were that protective. The idea of me having casual sex, the way most girls did in our pack, would have sent my father through the roof. He was always terrified that someone would hurt me."

Graves put down the bottle. "Are you saying you've never had sex?" He looked slightly aghast.

"I have. Why do you look like that?"

He cursed and went to the fridge, yanked it open to get another beer. "I made you get into my bed *naked*. My words were crude. That's why." He twisted off the cap and took a sip, closing the fridge door to stare at her. "I knew I was being an asshole, but if you were a virgin…" He growled, taking another drink. "I could have added traumatizing you to the list of mistakes I've made."

She nearly smiled but knew it would set him off. Graves was a good man. "I'm not traumatized. I know what oral sex is."

He relaxed his stiff stance.

"I've never had it or given it, but I've seen it on the internet. I also read books—"

The glass in his hand exploded, raining beer and pieces of the bottle to the floor. She stepped forward but he snarled, shooting her a glare that had her halting in her tracks.

He walked over to the sink, turning on the water. She spun, rushing to bedroom, where she knew a first-aid kit sat under the counter in the en suite. He had a dishtowel wrapped around his hand when she returned, picking up the largest pieces of glass from the floor.

"Let me get that."

"Stay the fuck back," he ordered.

She held the kit, watching him clean up the mess, his hand bleeding. It would stop soon, with his Werewolf healing ability, but she still had the urge to make sure no shards were stuck in his skin. The glass would eventually push its way out if he healed around any but it would be uncomfortable.

He finished cleaning the mess and threw the stained dishtowel into the trash, along with the glass he'd swept up and paper towels he'd used to mop the spilled beer. "You should go to your room. You know those bad days I mentioned? Today is one of them."

"You were on a job?" she guessed.

"I don't want to talk about it. Go to your room, Joni. Stay there. I'm going to get drunk and fall asleep." He went to the fridge to get another beer.

"You only have a few more in there. That won't do it. It takes a hell of a lot to get your kind wasted. I taught myself bartending on the internet...I can make some mixed drinks. It amused the enforcers. Would you like me to make something for you? I saw the hard liquor bottles in the cabinet over the fridge, when I was up on a chair cleaning."

He opened another beer and closed the fridge. This time he avoided looking at her. "You're being a shitty servant. I gave you an order. Follow it."

She probably should return to her bedroom, but instead she stepped closer. "Talking helps. Or hell...get mad and yell at me. Maybe that will help too."

He sighed.

"Tell me what you need, Graves. I'm here for you."

He took another sip of beer, just watching her. A good minute passed. She watched him back, waiting.

He finally glanced away. "Go. Trust me, it's safer for you."

Joni squared her shoulders and inhaled deeply. "Maybe I don't want to be safer."

He put the beer down and took a step toward her, then stopped. "Damn it, Joni! Not today. You want to stand up to me? Be all stubborn? Act like a little shit? Fine. Just not today. Not after the mess I've had to deal with. Go to your room."

"I don't believe you'd ever hurt me, Graves. You're a protector. Not an abuser."

He closed his eyes and leaned back against the island, his head hanging, hands gripping the edge of the counter on either side of his hips. She approached him, making sure he heard her coming closer. Werewolves had excellent senses and it was stupid to startle one. Especially a Were in a bad mood.

She stopped in front of Graves, reached out, and slowly wrapped her arms around his waist. He was a big man. She inched closer, turned her head, and pressed her cheek against his chest. It felt nice to hug him. She ignored the spots of wetness on his shirt from the incident with the exploding beer bottle.

She fully expected Graves to tear out of grasp, snarl, and raise hell. Instead, he stiffened...but as the seconds ticked by, his body slowly relaxed.

Minutes later, his arms circled her waist. Then he lowered his chin to rest on the top of her head.

He carried a wonderfully clean scent. There were no bad smells she could pick up from whatever he'd dealt with. It meant he'd showered recently, and that the clothes he wore must be clean ones. Even her human nose picked up laundry detergent and soap.

"Baby," he whispered huskily. "You need to get away from me or I'll try to lose myself in you."

"Whatever you need."

His body tensed briefly. "You don't know what you're saying."

"I belong to you. You're stuck with me. That doesn't mean we have to be miserable. Show me what you need. Or tell me. I'm right here."

He slid his hands down her back, resting them just above her ass. "Are you serious?"

"Yes. Whatever you want, Graves. I'm here for you."

"You've really *never* had oral sex?"

She felt a blush rise in her cheeks. "Out of everything I've said, that's what you want to talk about?"

"Yes. I can't wrap my head around it unless you're lying. You sure you're not a virgin? Be honest with me."

She liked this soft, husky tone of voice. "Not a virgin."

"Were you with humans or Weres? Both?"

"Human. Just one."

"Ah. That explains it." He softly chuckled.

She got the urge to look up at his face but he kept his chin firmly against the top of her head and his arms around her, holding her tightly. "It does?"

"They don't have our senses or needs. The other night, when I caught a whiff of your arousal, the first thing I wanted to do was get a taste and bury my nose right between your thighs to breathe you in. No self-respecting Were could just fuck a woman when she smells as good as you do. But our cocks are usually a lot bigger than humans'. Unless she's in heat, the wetter a human female gets, the easier it is to fit inside her without causing pain."

Her body responded to his sensual voice and the scenario he painted in her mind. She could imagine Graves between her thighs now, working his stiff cock inside her body. He'd be big. At least, if he were to be believed. She was willing to trust his word.

"I had to jack off three fucking times in the shower when I picked up your scent on my sheets, just to keep myself from going after you. The fact that you were ovulating made it worse. I don't have a mate, but I've noticed how good ovulating Werewolves smell just by being near them. Never repeat that I admitted that to you, though. No male wants to know other men are sniffing at their mates, but it can't be helped."

She had to swallow before speaking, desire making her throat feel dry. "I'll always keep your secrets."

One of his hands played with the hair that fell down her back. He lifted some of it, inhaling the strands. "You really should go to your room, Joni. Otherwise, there's a damn good possibility that you'll end up flat on your back in my bed with your legs wrapped around me. I'm a total bastard. After what happened the other night, how much I wanted you…I stopped to buy condoms. They're in my backpack over there."'

"Good." She was glad that he'd done that. "I'll go see a doctor as soon as possible to prevent getting pregnant, if you're willing to drive me there. I've heard that Werewolves hate using condoms."

He softly growled. "Joni."

"I'm here." She slowly released Graves and backed up. He let her go. She met his gaze. His eyes were that beautiful stormy blue-gray color and there was a wildness about the way he looked at her. He was extremely sexy right now.

"I'm willing. Grab the condoms. I'm going to go get naked in your bed."

He said nothing. Didn't move. Just watched her.

"Let me help you, Graves. Get lost in me. Please?"

His breathing increased and a low growl came from him. It was sensual when he licked his lips. "Run, baby. Last chance."

She smiled, understanding he meant to warn her off. She turned, rushing toward the stairs instead of to her bedroom, and ran right up to his room. There was no hesitation when she began to strip off her clothes. She might not be overly aggressive, but she'd made up her mind.

Heavy footsteps came up the stairs as she flung off the last of her clothes and lay down on his bed. Nervousness hit, but seeing Graves stalk into his room, carrying his backpack, distracted her from it.

His gaze traveled down her body and another growl came from his lips. He was almost panting as he tore open one of the side pockets of the bag, withdrawing a box of condoms. He tossed it at the end of the mattress and dropped the backpack.

"Don't say I didn't warn you."

His voice was gruff, more of a snarl than words, but she wasn't afraid of Graves hurting her.

She nodded. "Bring it." Then Joni smiled. *That* had been aggressive. Or at least, she hoped it sound that way to him.

Part of her couldn't believe it was really going to happen. She was in his bed, and Graves wasn't ordering her to leave. A little hope filled her that he wouldn't find her disappointing. Her experience with sex was sorely lacking. One of the downfalls of being a human raised by two very overprotective Werewolves.

* * * * *

Graves studied his sexy little human, his gaze roaming over every inch of her body. He wasn't sure if taking Joni up on her offer would kick him in the ass later, but at that that moment, he didn't care. Anything to blank out the images that haunted him from his most recent job.

An entire family had been wiped out, including four kids. He'd arrived too late to save any of them. Graves had taken out the two rogue Vampires who'd viciously killed them, and he'd also had to torch the home to hide the evidence of what had happened. Humans needed to believe they'd died in a tragic fire.

He stripped fast, his gaze now focused on Joni's face. She didn't appear afraid and when he inhaled, he didn't pick up the scent of fear. Only her arousal. It was faint…but he'd fix that fast. He wanted to taste her in the worst way.

His dick was already achingly hard. He took a moment to open the new box he'd tossed on the bed, removing a strip of condoms and tearing one off. He opened it, thinking it was better to be safe than sorry, if he forgot Joni was human once he'd put his hands and mouth on her.

The risk of pregnancy wasn't one he was willing to take. The only thing worse than him accepting responsibility for a woman was the idea of becoming a father. He wasn't fit for either. *Once, maybe. Not anymore.*

He rolled the condom over his dick and crawled onto the bed. Joni's gaze held his and he still didn't see any fear. She had a great body. Soft and shapely. Feminine. Human. That didn't turn him off. It just reminded him to be gentler than usual.

"Spread wider for me, baby."

She didn't hesitate to do as he'd demanded. Her nipples stiffened. He growled low as he got more comfortable on the bed and gently gripped her inner thighs, pushing them even farther apart.

He leaned in, inhaling her scent. Joni smelled so damn good, and he picked up that she was still ovulating. It was faint but there. The very idea almost made him lose control, Were instinct kicking in, and he wanted to fuck her so bad it actually hurt. Instead, he opened his mouth and ran his tongue over her pink clit.

Her gasp urged him on. He licked the little nub a few times, finding just the right pressure that made her moan his name. He liked the sound of that. Her arousal increased, the scent think in the air, and he felt how wet she was getting as he nuzzled in tighter, gently sucking on her clit.

"Graves!" she panted.

He glanced to the side, watching her hand frantically claw at the bedding. He wanted to feel Joni's fingernails dig into his back instead, but he needed to get her off first. He ran his tongue lower to get a better taste of her arousal.

His dick hardened to the point of agony and his balls throbbed. Joni tasted fucking delicious, the flavor made sharper by her ovulation. Were females only ovulated while mated, and even then only when they'd decided to breed. Instincts urged him to fuck her, hard, without a condom. He ignored his need and went for her clit again, merciless with his mouth as he stroked his tongue over and over against the swollen bud.

Joni thrashed on the bed and tried to close her legs. He refused to let her go and pinned her down tighter. Then she was crying out his name, jerking under him as she came, her sounds making Graves growl.

He pulled back, staring at her wet slit. She was ready for him. He released her thighs and straightened to his knees. "Look at me."

Joni opened her eyes, panting. He loved the way her features were flush with pleasure.

"Don't lie to me. You swear you're not a virgin?"

She shook her head. "I'm not."

"Good." Graves swiftly grabbed one of her legs and flipped her over, onto her stomach. She gasped but he ignored it, sliding off the end of the bed and yanking her with him, until they were both on their knees on his hardwood floor. He bent her over the end of the mattress, then grabbed her hips and pushed her a little higher, putting Joni exactly where he wanted her.

He stared down at her ass, his mouth watering. She had a great one, round and smooth. Graves used his knee to nudge her legs apart and released her hip to place one hand on her lower back. He gripped his condom-covered dick with the other, guiding his shaft to her. It almost broke his control when he brushed up against her wet slit.

"Are you ready for me, Joni?"

She nodded, her hands clutching the covers.

He began to push into her—and groaned. Joni was wet, but so fucking tight! A moan came from her as he paused, withdrew a little, then pushed in deeper. Her pussy fisted him like no other, and he hoped he didn't hurt her. She felt small, but she swore it wasn't her first time. He had to trust that.

He released his shaft and grabbed her hip, still pinning her with his other hand. He drove into her deeper. Joni moaned again, and he snarled as her body accepted more of his dick. She felt so damn good, her scent was urging him on. He began to thrust faster. She moaned even louder.

"Fuck," he snarled, pounding into her even as he shoved her bent form a little higher on the mattress.

He forgot everything but the feel and scent of Joni. How wet and warm she was. How good she felt. The sounds she made, her breathy pleas urging him to be a little rougher, lose some of his caution. "So fucking tight. So good!"

"Yes! I'm going to…"

He could tell as her pussy clamped around his dick. She cried out his name, her inner muscles spasming, clenching him over and over.

He drove into her deep and came hard. Ecstasy blasted through him and he groaned, his body quaking from the force of it.

He collapsed over her, but quickly remembered to brace his arms to keep from crushing Joni. A fine sheen of sweat made their bodies slide together. He liked the feel of it, liked having her under him as he tried to catch his breath and recover.

Graves had no urge to get off Joni, but he remembered the damn condom. He slowly withdrew his still-hard dick from her. Part of him regretted breaking the intimate contact as he stood and backed off.

"Climb to the center of the bed, on your back." He turned away and walked into his bathroom to dispose of the condom.

He returned to find Joni exactly where he'd told her to be. A little pink tinged her cheeks but she hadn't tried to cover her body. Her legs were closed, though. He stopped at the end of the bed, studying every inch of her. Then he climbed onto the bed. She blushed harder and lowered her gaze when he was level with her face.

"Joni? Look at me."

She hesitated but met his gaze.

"You're now fucking a Were. Get over your shyness—fast." He twisted on the bed, grabbed the roll of condoms, and tore off another. "Spread your legs. Don't hide from me. You're beautiful, baby, and the sight of you makes me so fucking hard." He waved a hand down at his dick. "See?"

She glanced down. "You're as big as you feel."

He grinned. "And you're as small and tight as I thought you'd be. It's been a few months since I've had sex. That was much faster than I'd intended. Now that the edge is off, spread your legs for me. This time it's going to be much slower."

She parted her legs, her sex glistening and swollen. He rolled on another condom and moved over her. Caging her with his body, he reached between them and used his thumb to play with her clit.

"Give me your throat," he demanded.

She didn't hesitate to twist her head, baring her smooth flesh. He groaned, kissing her skin. She tasted sweet. There was no perfume on Joni or traces of makeup. He felt his fangs slide down and didn't bother forcing them back up. She knew what he was. There was no reason to hide anything from the human in his bed. He nipped her lightly, and she moaned, grinding her pussy against his thumb.

He arched his back and lowered his head, going for her breast next. She had handful-sized tits with light pink nipples that were already puckered for him. He licked one, then ran his canines over the tight peak.

She arched her back, shoving more of herself into his mouth. His dick throbbed but he kept using his thumb to play with her clit. He alternated between her two breasts, licking and nipping until she was panting and pleading for him to take her.

Before he could even try, Joni came, crying out his name.

Graves pulled his thumb away from her clit and spread her legs wide. Then he was fucking her. She clutched at his shoulders, her fingernails lightly raking his skin, which he loved. He liked it even better when she wrapped her legs around his waist.

He growled. "Scratch me harder, Joni. You won't hurt me. Dig those nails in. I love how they feel." He began to thrust hard, taking her fast and deep.

Joni did as he asked. Her fingernails dug into his skin, giving him a bite of pain. It was just what he needed.

She was just what he needed.

He lowered his head, going for her throat again. He bit her, but not hard enough to draw blood. She wailed, the scent of her arousal doubling. He used his tongue to soothe the pain, then kissed her skin, growling in her ear as he continued moving inside her. She was so tight and hot. So wet. Fucking perfect.

He suddenly didn't mind having her in his space. Didn't mind taking care of her. Both were enjoyable as hell when she was in his bed.

Chapter Eight

Joni woke alone in bed. One glance at the clock on the nightstand showed it was after eight in the morning. It surprised her that she'd gotten so few hours of sleep because she felt so awake. The last time that Graves had woken her to have sex, the early rays of dawn had just broken through the windows of his bedroom.

She sat up and scooted to the edge of the bed, muffling a groan.

She was a bit sore. Her legs felt wobbly, too, when she stood. The thought of going downstairs had her heading into the attached bathroom instead. It was empty but a wet towel hung on the rack and the shower tiles were damp. Graves had used it. She peed and then stared at her reflection in the mirror.

There were some red marks on both sides of her neck and the tops of her shoulders. Graves liked to bite. She couldn't complain. It had felt amazing every time his teeth nipped her. The skin wasn't broken but she'd have light bruises.

Her hair was a tangled mess. That was from Graves too. He'd fisted handfuls of it a few times while he was inside her. She reached down to her oversensitive breasts and went up on her tiptoes to see them in the mirror. He'd left some red marks there too.

She dropped on the balls of her feet and visually inspected the rest of her body. There were more marks on the inside of her thighs. None of them hurt. Graves liked to put his mouth on her. Her only regret was that he'd not kissed her mouth.

It hurt her feelings a little, but he'd explained his interactions with women clearly. Graves didn't date or have relationships. He just fucked women and liked to walk away. None of them came to his cabin, he never took them in his own bed. Kissing probably wasn't on the table for his partners.

Graves had not only taken her on his bed, but he'd slept with her all night long. She'd fallen asleep cuddled against his side. He'd let her use his arm for a pillow. Maybe kissing on the mouth wasn't something he'd ever done? That seemed like a boyfriend/girlfriend kind of thing. Not that she was an expert.

She decided not to take it personal. The situation was new for them both. They'd have to figure it out how to proceed together. She could always try to kiss him next time. That would help her determine if he'd allow it or not.

She entered his shower, turning on the water. None of her things were in his bathroom but she mostly just wanted to rinse off. She'd deal with her hair later.

A soft groan came from her when she ran her hand between her legs to clean that area. She felt tender. No wonder. Graves had gone down on her four times, and they'd used *nine* condoms. It was a wonder she could even walk.

Joni closed her eyes, letting the warm water run over her face. She opened her mouth for a quick rinse. A toothbrush would be great, but that was down in her own bathroom.

She pulled away from the water, turned it off, and grabbed the already damp towel. She dried off and wrapped it around her body. It was time to go in search of Graves.

She really hoped the morning after wouldn't be awkward. They'd get through it regardless, because she was determined to make it work between them. She'd never been one for sex, not after her lackluster experience with another human...but one night in Graves's bed and she already didn't want to go back to sleeping in the guest bedroom.

Graves wasn't downstairs when she looked. She peeked outside to see his vehicle missing. Disappointment hit. He hadn't even left a note. Would he pretend the night before never happened? She wouldn't be surprised.

Joni entered her bedroom but left the door open. It was her way of giving him permission to come to her when and if he wanted. She went into her bathroom, brushed her teeth, and quickly washed her hair in her own shower. She finished and dried off, before getting dressed.

Graves didn't return after a good hour had passed. Doubts began to plague her. *Maybe he really will pretend like none of last night happened. Will he order me to leave? Maybe I shouldn't have pressured him. He could've at least left me a note saying where he went or when he'd be back.*

When she finally heard an engine, she walked into the kitchen. Seconds later, Graves unlocked the door and entered.

She forced a smile. "Hungry? It's nearly lunchtime."

He kicked the door closed behind him. "I ate a late breakfast."

She bit her lip, unsure what to say next, waiting to take her cues from him.

He walked over to the couch and sat down. "Come here."

She approached, feeling her heart pounding with dread. He didn't appear happy in the least. Definitely not anything resembling the hot, sexy guy who'd had his hands, mouth, and other body parts all over her during the night.

Joni sat where he indicated, which put a good foot and a half between them. Her gaze lifted to his face as he pinned her with a serious look.

"Are you sore?"

"A little. That's normal."

A muscle in his jaw jumped, and his expression turned grim. "I realized what I'd done when I saw you this morning. You're going to have bruises."

"It's okay."

He snarled.

The vicious reaction made her jump—which made him frown. "That was a scary sound, but I'm not afraid. You just startled me."

His eyes narrowed. "I marked you with my fangs."

"You didn't break the skin. I checked."

He growled low. "That's not the point. I told you my head was in a bad place."

"I know exactly where your head was through most of last night." She pointed at her lap. "Right down there." She smiled. "It was amazing."

Shock flashed across his face but he hid it fast. Graves blinked a few times, studying her closely.

"Are you about to say you regret what happened between us? Well...I don't. You can snarl, be grumpy, or even pretend it didn't happen. That's fine. Just know that I'm still here for you. To cook your meals or to sleep in your bed. Or *not* sleep." She winked.

"Who the fuck *are* you?" He still seemed stunned.

"Joni. Your servant. The one who's decided to call you on your shit. I've been worried since the moment I woke up alone, wondering what you'd say or do when you walked in the door. I know you left to avoid the whole morning-after scene."

He opened his mouth but no words came out.

She nodded. "Don't bother trying to deny it. We both know it. Maybe you woke up this morning and freaked out. Or you felt regret. Whatever it was, you bolted. That's fine. I get it. You're a loner. But you not only spent an entire night with me, we also shared your bed. You already said you don't allow anyone you fuck to enter your space, so I understand how difficult that must have been for you. But this approach? Insisting you've harmed me in any way, shape, or form? Is absolute bullshit."

"I *did* hurt you. You're going to have bruises."

"Stop. Rethink it, Graves. We did a lot of wonderful things last night. That probably freaks you out, and I'm right there with you, because it was a thousand times *better* than I imagined. My mom always warned me a Werewolf had mad sex skills. She was right. You've ruined me for humans forever, so congrats on that. And by *ruined me*, I mean you're all I'll ever want from now on. No one else. It was *that* good. You didn't hurt me. I'm sore because you're big, and it's been years since I've had sex."

His eyes widened.

"Um...I've only had sex twice, both in the same evening, with the same guy. That's when I lost my virginity. My parents were super overprotective, so I had to sneak away from my guard. It was at a party, shortly before I graduated from my human high school. He was a boy I liked, but he was really bad at it. *You* are amazing. I'll heal in no time and be ready for another round of what happened last night whenever you are."

Now he gawked at her. And the longer he said nothing, the angrier she became.

"But you just go ahead and continue to freak out. That's how you seem to deal with stuff that you aren't comfortable with. I'm learning that about you."

Joni stood, her voice rising, not caring that she was mouthing off to the man who basically owned her. "You need more time to process what happened between us? Fine, but you can't spin this into something bad. I won't let you, Graves. Just know that I don't expect anything from you. That's the part you don't seem to be getting. Just keep me safe, and in return, I'll be your servant. In bed, out of it...either way, I'm yours." She backed up a few steps. "I'll go to my room to give you space. If you want a meal, or chores done, or sex, come find me. If you want to flee your own home again, I'll be here when you get back. I'm not putting any pressure on you."

Joni forced herself to turn away and walk into her bedroom, softly closing the door, then climbing on her bed. Her heart continued to pound. Well...that started out okay, but then she'd lost her temper and let Graves have it.

Shit, she mouthed. A sense of "what did I just do" hit hard, but she couldn't change anything. Joni wasn't even sure if she'd want to. She'd meant every word.

Her gaze went to the door. Graves didn't storm in to yell at her. She heard only silence. The front door didn't slam, his boots didn't thump up the stairs.

Minutes later, she heard the fridge being opened and closed. Then the TV came on. He remained in the living room.

He hadn't taken off again. She'd count that as a win.

* * * * *

So Joni has a temper. Graves took a sip of soda, watching the television, and found himself smiling slightly. So much for the speech he'd practiced all morning, the one about how it wasn't safe for her to live with him.

He'd woken that morning to see red marks from the tips of his fangs that he'd left on Joni's delicate skin. He'd never marked a lover before. It had scared the shit out of him.

There was also the fact that Werewolf women healed fast. Bruises from rougher sex faded within an hour. Not on Joni. The marks he'd left on her might last for days or more.

He wasn't one to nip skin, either. That probably shocked him more than anything else. He kept his mouth closed during sex and his fangs far away from a woman's flesh. With Joni, he hadn't resisted the urge, and she'd seemed to love everything he'd done. She was very vocal with her pleasure.

He's stopped thinking entirely, once he got his hands and mouth on her. His mind had been in a bad place, and she'd let him forget everything while he got lost in her body. The sex was incredible. The fact that she was in his space, ovulating, and hell, she *belonged* to him...it all made everything scorching hot. The best fuck he'd ever given *or* gotten. He couldn't deny that.

Nor could he ignore the fact that he wanted her again. Right now.

At least he hadn't forgotten to use condoms.

That thought hit him like mental ice water and cooled his desire to go after her in her room. He couldn't fuck up that way. Micah would make a great father one day. Him, not so much.

He contemplated his past. He and his brother used to be so similar as kids, they got teased about being identical twins born a few years apart. Then, when he was a teen...that attack in the middle of the night happened.

Everything had changed.

Arlis's parents had been the alpha pair. There'd been no warning. The bastard from another pack who'd led the attack hadn't issued an alpha challenge. They'd snuck in like assassins, slaughtering anyone they found. One of the first homes they'd hit—after the alpha's—happened to belong to the father of his future mate. Graves had lost Londa and her entire family.

He became someone else after her death. It was simply how he'd dealt with the grief. Her family was murdered before he was even aware their territory had been invaded. The sound of loud howls and a few gunshots had woken him. At first, he'd assumed a group of humans had come to kill them. They were the ones who used guns to attack the packs.

He'd lost his mind when he'd made it to Londa's cabin and found her body.

That night, he'd taken his first life. And many more. He'd used his grief and fury to tear apart anyone responsible. By the time the sun had risen, there were no enemies left alive. Their land had been stained red with blood. The pack had lost their mated alpha pair and dozens of others to the attack.

Graves forced his thoughts out of the past, back to the present. Sometimes he looked at his fun-loving, easygoing younger brother and wondered if he'd have turned out like Micah as an adult, if he hadn't had his heart and his future ripped away.

Micah often talked about wanting a mate and kids. It was something his brother longed for, when he was ready to settle down. It wasn't a maybe; it was inevitable. Graves couldn't even fathom that now. No kid would want a killer for a dad. No woman would want him as a mate. He'd be shitty at both fatherhood and matehood.

His cell phone dinged in his pocket and he removed it, reading the text with a scowl. It was from Trent Blu.

The year before, Alpha Arlis had ordered Graves to check out a group of rogues after they'd claimed a section of territory around a small human town, almost an hour away by car.

He'd expected to have to take them out. Rogues were usually bad news. Especially if they grouped together. The ones who had the balls to send official notices to local packs that they'd claimed a territory were particularly vicious and nuts.

It was never good for humans when a group like that settled in. Rogues tended to terrorize their human neighbors. They might claim they were starting a pack, but most were just thugs who'd banded together to have strength in numbers.

That's not what Graves found when he'd gone to investigate. Instead, Trent Blu led a small group of former rogues who'd once belonged to shitty packs. They'd opened a legit business. Their main gig was private investigative work for humans. Trent had sworn they just wanted territory to call home, to live in peace, and would never hurt their neighbors, human or Were.

Graves had seen and sensed sincerity in the male. Trent was sane and reasonable. The guy also had alpha blood, strong enough that the male would have felt confident challenging Graves in a fight. That hadn't happened though. Trent hadn't done any posturing. He'd been respectful, polite, and had gone out of his way to answer all questions.

Graves had been leery. *If it sounds too good to be true...* That's why he'd stuck around for a full week, spying on the newly formed pack. He'd been impressed. Trent *did* run a legitimate business, and none of his pack mates were causing trouble. They were on the level. Mostly.

He *had* uncovered one lie...but once he realized why Trent hadn't mentioned the sixth member of his pack, he'd understood. Hell, he'd been even more impressed with their level of compassion. Most packs would have killed that particular shifter. Instead, Trent protected him.

Investigation complete, he'd reported to Arlis and the surrounding alphas that the newly formed pack wasn't a threat. He'd even thrown them some work, wanting them to succeed. When he was asked to track down any pack youths who decided to goof off with humans, he sent those jobs to Trent. They found the Were kids and returned them unharmed to their alphas.

Trent Blu: We got a job in your area. Runaway human off her medication. We were hired to find and return her to her people before she gets hurt or hurts someone else. Can you clear it with your alpha? We'll be in your town. She was spotted near there.

Graves texted back, acknowledging the info, and told Trent that would be fine. Then he shot off a text to Arlis. His alpha responded that he'd send out notice to everyone. No one wanted to mistake alliance pack members for rogues.

He put away his phone and leaned his head back on the couch, his thoughts returning to Joni. No way could he mess up by getting her pregnant. That meant either taking her to their pack healer or never touching her again. Condoms could break.

The state of his semi-hard dick just *thinking* about her made the decision for him. He stood. "Joni?"

She came out of her bedroom, leaning against the doorframe. He hated to see the way she looked at him. Like she was bracing for bad news. "Yes?"

"I heard every word you said. I *am* freaking out. What if one of those condoms I used had broken, or I'd forgotten to put one on? I don't want to become a father. I'm gone too much, and you know what I do for a living. Are you willing to go see our healer?"

She pushed away from the doorframe and nodded. "Of course."

He felt a little guilty that this was all on her. "I'd offer to get snipped, but…"

"You'd heal. I know how it works." She flashed him a brief smile. "Vasectomies on your kind don't stick."

"I'll call Marco first to see if he can help you. We had Shay living with us, which meant our healer was equipped to handle human issues, since she mostly took after her mother."

"Had? Shay isn't part of your pack anymore?"

"She found her mate and left with Trayis."

Tension marred her features. "Your alpha asked her to go? He wouldn't accept her mate into your pack?"

Graves shook his head. "It wasn't like that. Shay's mate happened to be Arlis's older half-brother. Trayis leads a VampLycan clan in Alaska. He's the equivalent of being their alpha."

Joni's eye widened. "Wow. I hadn't heard that."

Her surprise amused him. "Most people are too smart to gossip about VampLycans."

"That's how you're linked to the VampLycans? I mean, packs know you have an alliance with them, but they don't know how that came about. Can I ask…" She sealed her lips. "Never mind."

He studied her. "You said you'd keep all my secrets. Did you mean that?"

"Absolutely."

Graves stared into her eyes, already knowing he could trust her. "You're a part of the pack now. That means keeping pack secrets, too. What do you want to know?"

"So…the VampLycans made an alliance with your pack solely because your alpha is related to one?"

"Yes. There are other packs who have the same type of alliances with them due to family bonds. There's even a pack I sometimes visit that's related to the GarLycans. Their clan members would go to battle to protect those particular Weres."

Her eyes widened again. "Have you ever met any GarLycans?"

He smiled over her astonishment. "Yes. I sometimes do favors or jobs for them and the VampLycans."

Joni didn't disappoint when more surprise registered on her face at that tidbit. "You judge for them?"

"No. They handle their own internal problems. I've helped them find certain targets who were causing problems, or got them things they needed help acquiring. VampLycans and GarLycans sometimes intervene when trouble is brewing, if it's something a pack can't easily handle. Like when a large, aggressive Vampire nest needs taken out."

"Wow."

He cleared his throat, getting back on track with the conversation. "I'll find out if our pack healer can help us. I won't risk getting you pregnant."

Joni lowered her gaze from his. "I understand."

His phone cell rang and he pulled it out, glanced at the screen, then answered. "What is it?"

"A job came in," Arlis informed him. "The Brine pack alpha needs an enforcer judged immediately."

Dread filled Graves. He knew that pack. They were about a hundred miles away. He'd worked with them three years before, when they had four juveniles go missing. The teens were found alive but had been held captive by a Vampire nest. "Which enforcer, and what crime is he accused of?"

"*Her* name is Emily. Do you know her?"

Brown hair, big green eyes, and a wide smile flashed through his thoughts. "Yeah. I do. She's not a troublemaker."

"Apparently, she killed someone popular in the pack." Arlis paused. "She's claiming self-defense, but the dead male's family is saying it was in retaliation because he refused to mate her. It's a powder keg about to go off. Chip wants an outsider to deal with this so he's not accused of favoritism. Between you and me, I got the impression he didn't care for the one who died. I can see why he'd want you to step in."

"Me too. Emily is also the alpha's cousin. Did Chip mention the name of the male she killed?"

"Zander."

More memories came to him. "I remember him, if he's the only one with that name. Total asshole. One of the missing kids I helped find happened to be his younger brother. I damn near beat the shit out of him when he berated the kid for getting taken by a nest. Like a ten-year-old should have been able to fight off Vampires. Tell Chip I'm on my way."

"I'll let him know." Arlis disconnected.

Graves returned his phone to his pocket.

"You have to go. I heard." Joni gave him a nod. "Be careful."

He approached her. "I'm hoping I'll be back sometime tonight. I have a feeling this is going to be an easy judging gig."

Curiosity flashed in her eyes. It made him smile when she didn't ask questions, even though he'd bet she really wanted to. "I'll call our pack healer during the drive. Feel free to sleep in my room if I'm not back by the time you go to bed."

Joni smiled at him, nodding.

He turned away, rushing up the stairs to grab his backpack. He probably wouldn't need spare clothing but he always had them on hand just in case. There was no telling if he'd get bloody or not when he went to work.

Chapter Nine

Graves was in a bad mood when he parked his SUV in the Brine pack territory's car lot and climbed out of the driver's seat. The phone conversation he'd had while driving had pissed him off.

Marco, the pack healer, had flat-out refused to put Joni on birth control pills or insert an IUD. The coward didn't have the guts to touch a woman living under Graves's roof. That would mean having to take her to a human doctor. He didn't like that idea.

He strode into the Brine pack office but didn't have to ask to see Chip. The alpha waited for him just inside the door. Graves noticed the stress in his green eyes and the tension in his body.

"Thank you for coming, Judge."

Graves glanced around, a little surprised that no one else seemed to be in the office. Most alphas tended to keep a few of their enforcers nearby when an outsider came visiting. Then again, Graves had been there before. "I take it that you wanted to speak to me alone?"

"I've got a bad situation happening," Chip admitted. "Zander was popular with the pack but a known pain in my ass. His death is stirring up trouble."

"Arlis gave me some details. Emily is family to you, and she's one of your enforcers. You give them authority to dole out punishment if the need arises, but now someone is dead. Her justification is in question. Is the dead guy the same one who yelled at that ten-year-old from the Vampire kidnapping?"

Chip appeared surprised. "You remember him? Yes, it's the same Zander. Apparently, he's been harassing Emily. She didn't say anything to anyone because she worried it would make her appear weak."

Graves agreed. "Some of your males are probably resentful that you made her one of your enforcers. Idiots don't see females as worthy or strong enough to hold that position. They would have held it against her if she'd complained and maybe even bullied her into stepping down from the position. Was that why Zander was harassing her? Did he possibly feel he might have won the spot if she hadn't?"

"Zander never stood a chance of becoming an enforcer. He's always been ambitious but he doesn't have the temperament for that much responsibility. I'd been very clear to him about why he'd never advance far in the pack. He's a hothead and tends to be petty, so I had him assigned as a scout. He repeatedly fucked that up by literally sleeping on the job or not showing up for his shifts. I switched him to landscaping duty under supervision. I couldn't even trust Zander to cut the grass without someone looking over his shoulder."

"So his beef was with you? Do you think Zander went after Emily as payback for being treated like a youth because he's an irresponsible shithead?"

Some of the tension left Chip when his lips twitched. "Pretty much."

"Did Emily just finally have enough of his shit and lose her temper?"

Anger flickered in the alpha's eyes. "I told you that he could be petty, but he also had a mean streak. Zander thought he could take Emily in a fight and force a mating."

Graves's surprise was quicky followed by fury.

"He punched my cousin in the face without warning. She didn't even see him coming. She fell, and Zander probably thought he'd knocked her out. Then the prick began to tear at her clothes, saying he'd make her his bitch, then I'd have to give him a cushy job since we'd be family." Chip growled low. "He'd only stunned her when he broke her jaw. Emily *did* lose her temper, but he was attempting to rape and bite her at the time. So she killed him."

"Good." Graves crossed his arms. "Who's disputing the justification?"

"Zander has three older brothers who are a lot like him, and they got that from their father. Everything is always someone else's fault instead of them taking responsibility for their own actions. When they hear something they don't like, all of them have been known to twist the truth into a lie they like better. Apparently, Zander had been telling them that Emily wanted him to mate her." Chip rolled his eyes.

"What's the real problem? It's basically he said, she said. This shouldn't even be in dispute."

"Zander's family all have big mouths and they're circulating bullshit. Emily's taste in lovers hasn't always been the best. She had a crush on Zander as a youth, but that was over ten years ago, until she realized he was a loser. I don't think she ever slept with him, but there's a slim chance she might have back then. I try hard not to know anything about my cousin's sex life. The pack has a long memory though. There're also some who resent that I made Emily an enforcer. Not that they question her skills or strength. She earned that position."

"Every pack has assholes who want to make a mountain out of a molehill. They probably speculate that Emily was made an enforcer because of nepotism."

Chip nodded. "It's not true. She's one tough bitch with a level head. I need a clear-cut judgement from you. That way, no one can accuse me of letting her get away with murder. Zander might have been a shithead and lazy, but he was liked by enough of the pack to cause trouble if they buy into the story that Emily murdered him out of revenge for not mating her." Anger flashed in the alpha's eyes.

"Understood. I take it there were no witnesses to what happened between the two?"

"No. Zander jumped her in a remote area."

"Where is Emily and Zander's family now? I'd also like to see the body."

"I had my enforcers secure the scene. Emily was ordered to remain there. I didn't allow her to change clothing or even wash her hands. I was hoping you were available and could come quickly. Not only are you the closest judge, but I know you're fair. You won't hold it against my enforcer for having breasts. Thank you for coming right away."

"Lead me to the location."

Graves followed Chip out of the office. He knew when they were close to the scene since he heard voices. The dirt path in the thickly wooded area dipped down into a shallow ravine. He got his first glimpse of what waited.

Over two dozen pack members had gathered on one hillside overlooking the dead body. Four male enforcers were spaced out at least thirty feet from where it lay. Emily stood alone, about ten feet from the body. He took in her appearance.

Blood had dried on her lips and trailed down her jaw and throat to stain her ripped T-shirt. The damage to the material was significant on one shoulder, the reason why her breast on that side was mostly exposed. There was more blood on her hands. Especially her right one. It was totally soiled. Her shoulders were squared, her features stoic, and he also noticed the state of her pants. The zipper of her jeans was open, exposing a hint of bright blue panties. A few leaves were stuck in her messy hair.

He bypassed Emily without uttering a word, taking his focus off her. He motioned for the Brine alpha to back off as he walked directly to the body. Graves crouched about five feet away, visually examining the ground around it. The dirt was disturbed and the dry foliage crushed, evidence that supported a struggle had taken place.

Next, he glanced up the hillsides that flanked the narrow ravine, then the area protected by the enforcers, noting the places where someone could remain hidden. The best spot was on the hillside to his right, close to where he now crouched.

Chip had said Emily hadn't seen the attack coming. He'd check that spot next, but it's where he'd have chosen if he'd planned an ambush.

He inched closer to the body and inhaled. The breeze and time had eradicated any evidence he might find by smell. That was the bad thing about someone dying outside. He carefully turned the body face up and immediately saw what had killed Zander. Graves was impressed. Emily had ripped out his throat with her claws. That accounted for all the blood covering her right hand and staining the ground beneath the body. Zander had died face down in the dirt.

Graves examined Zander's hands. A quick death wouldn't have allowed him to heal. He found blood on the right hand and damaged knuckles, indicating Zander had hit something with great force. He pressed against the male's fingertips, feeling the tips of his claws barely beneath the surface. They'd started to retreat under the skin while Zander was dying, but didn't get far.

He scanned the rest of the body. The Were's pants were unfastened, and there was no damage to the material. Nor were there traces of blood on the fabric or his skin in that region.

Some parts of his job, he really hated. Like checking to see if the body was going commando. It was. Zander only wore pants, which would have made it easier to access his dick if he'd planned to rape a woman. To be fair, it could also mean the male just hated wearing underwear.

He pulled down the male's shirt to cover the front of Zander's open pants and stood.

The hillsides were steep. Graves carefully picked his way about eight feet up to a large boulder, partially hidden by an even bigger shrub. It didn't take a genius to find where someone had crouched down to wait. From the crushed leaves and imprints in the dirt, he knew someone had been on their hands and knees, waiting to spring an ambush. The imprints of the hands alone implied it was someone large enough to have been Zander. Not Emily.

He turned his head, studying the rest of the hillside. Light tracks were visible from the top of the hill, ending near the boulder. Two particular footprints were very distinct. They were large, also implying a male. He glanced at Emily, just to be sure. She had much smaller feet.

He finally approached Emily. She stiffened but lifted her chin, meeting his gaze. He saw a flash of dread, maybe even fear, but she held steady. He respected her courage. Most people feared him just because of his job. They tended to get the urge to run from the predator they sensed inside him, or at least flinch and cower. Right now, her life was in his hands. They both knew it.

He stopped before her. "I need to examine you. You're technically evidence. Will you permit it? I'm going to have to touch you." He lowered his voice. "I'll be as respectful as possible. Everything I do is for a reason."

"Of course." Her voice came out steady.

Graves didn't miss the way she tensed up even more, though. He didn't blame her, especially after what he believed she'd recently endured. He moved closer, leaning in to examine her face. She'd mostly healed, but he could still make out faint signs of bruising on her skin. He could tell where she'd been punched with a closed fist, and while her lip had healed, the dried blood told him it had probably been split upon impact.

He reached out and adjusted her torn shirt, examining it closely as well. It bothered him that her breast was exposed to the pack against her will, even though she wore a somewhat modest bra.

He stepped around her, moving her hair with one hand. He could see where her shirt had been ripped and found a few dried blood marks on her skin. Those injuries had healed as well, but claws had obviously dug into the shirt, leaving four streaks of blood starting at her shoulder and trailing down her back.

He crouched behind her, examining tears at the waist of her jeans. Also consistent with a clawed hand puncturing the material.

Emily jerked slightly when he slid a single finger into the damaged waist of her jeans and pulled back slightly, taking a peek inside. Her panties were torn at the top, with more dried blood on her skin and the material, evidence additional healed injuries. Graves released the material.

Returning to her front, he crouched again. He hesitated, hating this part. "I'm going to examine your pants in the front. Forgive my touch."

Emily peered down at him. "He tried to get them down. He didn't."

"Quiet, please. I'll ask questions if I need to." Graves lowered his gaze to her open jeans. The buttonhole was torn and the zipper broken. He could picture exactly what must have happened. A clawed hand had grabbed the back of her pants and used enough force trying to jerk them down, causing the damage to the front. It had to have hurt, having claws tearing into not only the material, but her skin.

Graves got back to his feet and met her gaze. "Did he get more than just his claws into your pants?"

Tears welled in her eyes but Emily blinked them back fast. "He didn't."

Relief filled him. The dead bastard hadn't physically hurt her worse than the damage he'd mentally cataloged.

Graves backed up, glancing at the enforcers securing the scene before turning back to Emily. "Of those who aren't mated, which of your fellow enforcers do you trust the most?"

Uncertainty showed in her eyes, but her gaze went to a tall blond. Graves motioned for that enforcer to come forward. The blond glanced at his alpha for permission before striding toward Graves.

"Give her your shirt," he ordered. "She's not evidence anymore. There's no longer a need for her to stand here exposed."

He didn't wait to see if the enforcer followed his order. He turned and studied the increasing crowd gathering on the hillside. It didn't take him long to locate Zander's family. The father had very strong genes, since all his sons looked just like him. He stalked toward them.

The father stepped forward to meet him. "That bitch murdered my son! I want to be the one to kill her."

Graves snarled, his anger obviously overwhelming the other Werewolf, who instantly lowered his gaze and stepped back. He knew the male was grieving and upset, but no one was permitted to forget that Emily's fate was up to him.

"Who was Zander's closest friend?"

The father's head snapped up. "What does that have to do with anything? He was my son! It's my right to seek vengeance."

"No. It's *mine*. Now answer me." Graves allowed some of his alpha vibes to flow.

The male instantly backed down yet again, shoulders and head drooping. The father stumbled back another step before turning his head, looking at a Were with long hair pulled back in a ponytail.

"You." Graves pointed at that male, then to the spot in front of him.

The Were looked like he wanted to flee. Graves narrowed his eyes and pointed to the ground again. The Were came to him slowly. When he finally reached the spot, the male's body language broadcasted his fear.

"Do you know who I am?"

The male nodded. "You're Graves."

"So you've heard stories about me?"

The male nodded and swallowed so hard, it was audible.

"Then you know I detest liars. I can sense when someone is being dishonest. Look at me. You *will* tell me the truth. I bet you and Zander talked a lot, didn't you?"

The male nodded and the scent of terror began to pour off him.

"That's what I thought. Whose idea was it—yours or his?"

The stink of his fear increased, sweat broke out on the male's face, and his hands started to shake.

Graves suddenly grabbed him by his ponytail and yanked his head back. The male whimpered. "Was it your idea or Zander's?"

The male kept silent.

"*Answer me,*" Graves roared.

"I told him it wasn't going to work!" the male blurted. He squeezed his eyes closed and nearly crumpled to the ground. He would have, if Graves wasn't still clutching his hair.

Graves shoved him away hard, and the Were landed on his ass. "Do not move or I'll break both of your legs."

"What are you doing? Leave Brian alone!"

Graves snarled at Zander's father. "Getting the truth. Which is already obvious to me." He bent and grabbed the terrified Were on the ground by his throat. He could sense his decision to run; he wasn't about to let him. "Tell them Zander's plan, Brian."

The male whimpered.

"Tell them," Graves demanded, deepening his tone enough to make everyone around watching flinch.

"He said he'd knock her out and she'd wake up mated to him," the male whispered.

"Louder," Graves demanded. "And be clearer. Use names."

"Zander said he'd knock Emily out and by the time she woke up, she'd be his mate. Then the alpha would have to take him back as a scout," the male sobbed loudly. "He was really pissed about having to rake leaves and pick up trash. I *told* him it was a bad idea! He wouldn't listen. He was too mad!"

"Was Emily chasing after him?"

The Were shook his head. "No. She kept telling him to fuck off and leave her alone," he choked out.

Graves released the male and straightened. He curled his lip and glared at everyone assembled on the hill. "That settles who was harassing whom. Forcing a mating is a death sentence. I would have come here to kill Zander myself if he'd succeeded."

He almost felt bad for Zander's family. *Almost.* They had to have known the Were had a flawed sense of honor.

"All the evidence speaks clearly." He pointed up the opposite hillside. "Zander waited behind that boulder and ambushed your pack enforcer. His claws damaged her skin and clothing, and she defended herself against a heinous crime. The death was justified—even merciful. Emily granted him a quick death. I would have made him suffer first, if he'd attempted to rape and force me into a mate bond.

"That's my ruling. It was self-defense."

No one argued. Not even Zander's father. That male turned away, fleeing. His remaining sons followed. A few of the less timid pack members nodded at Graves when he met their gazes.

He returned to Emily, who now wore the blond enforcer's shirt. Graves reached out and gently grasped her shoulder. "I deem you innocent of any crime," he stated. Then he released her, turning to Chip. "You have my ruling, Alpha Chip. Your enforcer's actions were justified and warranted."

"Thank you, Judge."

Formalities over, Graves walked away from the scene. He heard someone follow and glanced back. Chip flashed him a smile and caught up to him, lowering his voice.

"I can't thank you enough. I knew Emily was in the right but..."

"Now there's no doubt."

"How did you guess that Zander had told Brian what he was going to do?"

"Because I know the type of asshole he was. They like to brag and share their moronic plots with their even stupider friends. Zander couldn't keep his mouth shut the last time I met him. People like him never change."

"I'm surprised Brian spilled his guts so easily." The alpha sighed heavily. "Some of the pack will shun him for not immediately notifying me or an enforcer about a plan to force a mating."

That didn't concern Graves. The jerk deserved it. "My reputation tends to make *everyone* talk. It's hard to think up a lie when you're trying not to shit your pants or puke."

Chip chuckled. "Please stay for dinner if you can. I know Emily would like to thank you again, once she's showered and changes clothes." The male grew somber. "I'd appreciate it if you'd stick around to talk to her. She's very shaken up, even though she tried to hide it. This wasn't her first kill, but she grew up with Zander. And it's even worse because her word was questioned and some of the pack listening to his bullshit. Maybe you could give her advice on how to handle it. You deal with a lot of packs, including others with female enforcers."

Graves wanted to immediately go home to Joni, but he knew spending a few more hours in the Brine territory would be the right thing to do. Especially if he could make the aftermath of Emily's ordeal any easier to handle. Life was rough on female enforcers. She needed all the encouragement he could offer to prevent her from stepping down.

"I'll stay for dinner and talk to Emily. Then I need to leave. Would you consider having whoever prepares your meals do it a little earlier than normal?" He wasn't about to share why. Chip might ask questions about

Joni. That was something he wanted to avoid until he knew what the hell he was doing with her, himself.

"Of course," Chip agreed. "Does four o'clock work for you?"

"Yeah." He'd make it home before dark and get to spend the evening with Joni.

Chapter Ten

Joni stood at the sink, washing the pan she'd used earlier to cook a grilled cheese sandwich for her late lunch, when the cabin door slammed. She turned, expecting to see Graves—and gaped as she watched a woman with wavy blonde hair twisting the lock on the front door.

The stranger spun around and smiled wide, advancing on her quickly. "Hi! I'm Mandy. Graves is my son. You can call me mom if you'd like. You're family now."

Joni turned off the water in the sink and blindly reached for the dishtowel to dry her hands. Micah had warned her about possibly seeing their mother. "Um, hello."

The blonde stopped just a few feet away. She appeared to be about thirty, way too young to have two adult sons, which was normal with Werewolves. They aged much slower than humans. Her own adopted mother didn't look old enough to have a grown daughter, either.

Mandy was a few inches shorter than Joni. It stunned her, since she'd never met an adult Were smaller than herself. Graves's mother had sky-blue eyes and delicate features. Her blonde hair was very pale and flowed almost to her waist.

"You are adorable!" Mandy reached out and gently gripped Joni's arms. "How are you doing? Graves told me a little bit about your situation." Her happy expression faded. "You poor thing. Your parents must have been desperate to give you to my son. But he's a good male. You can count on Graves taking very good care of you and being an excellent provider. His bark is way worse than his bite. And you're not alone. You have all of us now."

Joni managed to nod, still shocked by a visit from Graves's mother. "I could have sworn I locked the door."

"Oh, you did. I have a key." Mandy grinned and tapped her pocket, where keys jingled. "Tell me everything about you! I want to hear—"

A loud pounding started on the front door, and a deep male voice bellowed from outside. "Let me in!"

Joni instantly froze in fear.

Mandy released her and turned away. "Go away, Angelo!" She glanced back at Joni and winked. "My mate is pissed that I tricked him."

"Babe, you promised our son!" the male argued.

Mandy snorted and stalked toward the front door, twisting the lock and yanking it open. She put her hands on her hips and glared up at a tall, dark-haired Were who...

Wore only a towel around his hips and an angry expression on his face?

"You didn't get dressed before coming after me? Really, Angelo. No wonder you got here so fast. I thought I had a few more minutes."

The angry Were tried to grab Mandy by the arm but she leapt back, surprisingly fast for someone her size, and hissed at him. "You're not taking me home yet! I made it here before you could stop me, fair and square. I *told* you I wanted to meet Joni. Nobody stops me when my mind is set. Now go upstairs to put on some clothes while I get to know this beautiful girl. You and Graves are about the same size." Mandy turned back to Joni. "This is my mate and the father of both my sons. Say hello, Angelo."

The tall Were growled low but gave a nod to Joni. "It's nice to meet you. We're sorry for barging in. As you can hear, my mate really wanted to see you, but we'll be leaving now. Babe, let's go."

Mandy dodged out of his reach again when Angelo entered the cabin and tried to snatch her hand. The much shorter woman darted around the couch to put it between them and growled. "I'm staying."

"Our son is going to be pissed." Angelo shot Joni an apologetic look before scowling at his mate. "Graves said he wasn't ready for you to meet her yet."

"Well, I'm *more* than ready. I'm tired of Graves having his head up his ass. Consider it pulled out now. Now go grab something to wear. I can't believe you chased after me in a towel."

"*I* can't believe you had me run a bath while you said you'd make us snacks, then instead of joining me, you ran out the back door as soon as I started the water! That's just mean."

"We'll share that bath tonight. Right now, Joni needs to know she has us in her corner. Graves is wrong to keep her all to himself. She's his, which makes her ours too." Mandy flashed another smile at Joni. "Family is very important, and that's exactly what we are."

"Thank you." Joni tried not to laugh, now that she was no longer frightened. She liked Graves's mother, even if she was a little crazy. At least it was in a good way. Mandy was very different from her serious son.

"I'm inviting you to dinner tonight, since Graves was sent off on a job. Darlene—she works in the pack office—told me he's in Brine territory, which is at least an hour and a half away. You'll come, of course." Mandy beamed at her.

That had Joni shaking her head reluctantly. "Graves doesn't want me to leave his home."

"Pish!" Mandy rolled her eyes. "Sweetie, I'm going to give you the advice I'd give my own daughter, if I had one. That's how I'm thinking of you from now on. Males hate it when their females do everything they say. They need a challenge."

"I wouldn't agree with that," Angelo huffed. "I'd love it if you actually did what I told you to for once."

Mandy spun toward him. "You *love* a challenge! It's why I'm such a wonderful mate for you. I never let you get bored, Angelo."

"That's one way to put it." He snorted.

Joni hid a smile.

Mandy turned back to her. "You're coming home with us, and I'll make you dinner. What are your favorite foods?"

"I eat just about anything, but I really can't leave." Joni was tempted, but the last thing she wanted was to make Graves mad. They were finally getting along, and he wasn't attempting to get rid of her anymore. That could change on a dime.

"I'll take the blame. My sons know how I am. Graves will understand. I promise." Mandy waved at her mate. "Upstairs. Clothes. No way are you walking home looking that sexy. I don't want Joni here to see me beating some bitch's ass for staring at my eye candy. I'm trying to make a good first impression."

"Good luck with that after this stunt, babe." Angelo headed toward the stairs obediently. The door closed above, she assumed to Graves's bedroom.

Mandy grinned and held out her hand. "Come here, sweetie."

She didn't hesitate. This was Graves's mother, after all. Joni crossed the room and clasped her hand.

Mandy immediately spun and dragged her to the front door. Joni opened her mouth to ask where they were going, but the shorter Were silenced her by pressing a finger to her lips. Mandy unlocked the door and yanked it open, tugging her outside.

There was an open-top Jeep waiting where Graves normally parked his SUV. Mandy hurried toward it, releasing her hand. "Get in, quick!"

Joni hesitated.

"Hurry! I told you, men don't like us being too predictable."

Joni rounded the Jeep and climbed into the passenger seat. "You don't want your mate to drive to your home with us?"

"He'll just lecture me the entire way," Mandy muttered, starting the engine. "Hang on!" She threw it in reverse and backed out fast.

Joni fumbled for the seat belt since there wasn't a door, using her other hand to grab at the bar attached to the dash in front of her. Mandy drove like a lunatic, hitting the brakes hard to complete her turn, then punching the gas.

"Are we racing your mate home?" Joni got the belt fastened but kept a firm grip on the bar in front of her. She really didn't like not having a door. The wind blew her hair into her face, since there was no roof, either, and she couldn't see.

"Oh, he'll beat us." Mandy flashed another big smile. "We're going to the store. Angelo would've pitched a fit if I'd even suggested taking you with me, but you've got to have cabin fever by now. Besides, I didn't actually think I'd get the chance to sneak out." She laughed. "I only thawed out a five-pound bag of shrimp for dinner. We can do much better than that for your first family meal. What's your favorite dish of all?"

"I really do eat almost anything. Um, is this store in your pack territory?"

"We have one, but by this time of day all the good meats will be gone. We're going human. I love shopping there. They have so much more to offer."

Joni figured Graves was going to kill them both. "I really don't think we should leave your territory…"

"No worries. We've got pack operating in town. Did some of your old pack infiltrate the police department and stuff to keep an eye on the local humans?"

"Yes." Joni watched them drive at a high rate of speed down a paved road, passing a few cabins. It wasn't the road Graves had driven on when he'd brought her home. "I like shrimp. We should just have that for dinner."

"Angelo will eat most of it himself. That mate of mine can really pack away food. I'm sure you've learned that, living with Graves. I'll invite Micah to come, too. A real family dinner. You should get to know your brother."

Joni opened her mouth but she truly had no clue how to respond to that. Mandy was acting like she was Graves's mate. She very much wasn't, but she decided to let him deal with his mother when he got home. The last thing she needed was to start an argument with the woman who'd birthed him.

Mandy slowed once they passed an open gate. Joni twisted in her seat, seeing the warning signs posted on the fences on either side of the road, stating that it was private property. She also glimpsed a few cameras. "Is this the back entry into your territory?"

"One of them. We have a few. This one is a shortcut into town. You might see some scouts. Just wave to them if you do."

Joni studied the woods, not spotting anyone. "Am I even allowed to go anywhere? I mean, Graves said your alpha wouldn't let him take me to the airport."

Mandy slammed on the brakes, bring the Jeep to a sudden stop on the two-lane paved road. It was hard enough to toss Joni against the seat belt. She gaped at Mandy. The other woman stared back with narrowed eyes.

"Why was my son going to take you to the airport?" She growled the words, her anger clear.

No way did Joni want to throw Graves under the bus with his mother. "I felt so guilty about being dumped on your son that I offered to leave," she lied.

Mandy's features softened. "You're such a sweetheart." Her smile returned. "You're not a prisoner. You're family. Of *course* we can go shopping together. It's what mothers and daughters do." Mandy took her foot off the brake and they were off again, heading down the road.

It seemed that Joni was going into town. Not that she had a choice. She just hoped Graves would realize none of it was her fault. The only alternative would be to jump from the moving vehicle and make her way back to his home. She wasn't about to upset his mother by doing something drastic.

Something Joni's own mother always told her came to mind. *Pick your battles wisely.* It was good advice in this situation. It was never a good thing to upset the mother of the man you lived with.

Fifteen minutes later, they were parking in the lot of a large grocery store, and Joni had to admit...it did feel good to be out and about.

* * * * *

"Some males are going to do really stupid things. It's never easy for a female to have your position. Idiots can't wrap their heads around it, and that's their problem. What happened wasn't your fault. I'm betting a lot of young females admire and look up to you for being brave enough to become an enforcer. Focus on that," Graves advised Emily.

"Have you met a lot of female enforcers?"

"I have. They deal with assholes all the time, people who believe that only males should be enforcers. Stand up to anyone who gives you shit. That's the best revenge. You kick their ass and show them why you've earned your position."

"Listen to Graves," Chip encouraged. "You did earn your spot. Remember when Don challenged you to a fight because he felt he deserved to be promoted? He got his ass kicked pretty badly. You may be smaller, but you're meaner and a more skilled fighter."

Emily nodded, the tension in her expression easing. Graves was glad he'd decided to stick around to talk to her.

Dinner was served, and he'd shared a few stories of some of the other female enforcers he'd met when his cell chirped with a text. He pulled it out and glanced at the screen.

The words didn't register for a split second—but then they did.

He stood fast and held Chip's gaze. "I apologize, but I need to cut dinner short."

The alpha also rose to his feet. "A problem? Is there anything we can do to help?"

"I've got this." Graves glanced at Emily and gave her a nod before leaving the pack's clubhouse. He dialed his father as he hurried toward the parking lot, where he'd left his SUV. His dad answered immediately.

"Mom kidnapped Joni? What the hell, Dad? What does that even mean?"

"Your mom said she was going to make some snacks to feed me in the bath—"

"I don't want to hear anything related to that. Get to the part about Joni."

"I was just climbing into the tub when I heard your mom's Jeep squeal out of the driveway. I knew where she was heading. I ran to your place, but she was already with Joni."

"So Mom's at my cabin?" He relaxed and slowed his pace. "You said *kidnapped*. You meant Mom invaded my home and…what? Is she interrogating Joni?"

"I went upstairs to your bedroom to put on some pants, and that damn mate of mine fled again! She took your human with her. I thought they'd be here at the house, but they weren't. I pulled up the tracker I installed, and they're on their way into town."

A snarl burst from Graves, and he started to jog toward his SUV. "Pants? I'm not even going to ask. What are they going to town for?"

"I don't know," his father snapped. "There's no figuring out your mother. She does what she wants. I was gonna jump in my truck to go after them but my keys are gone. Mandy must have hidden them. That's when I sent a text to you, then Micah. He's coming to get me and we'll go after them. *This* is why I installed that damn tracker on your mother's Jeep. She's going to drive me insane!"

"I'm on my way home."

"Finish your job first. Micah and I will wrangle your mom and get Joni back to your cabin. I just wanted to let you know what was going on."

"I'm coming home *now*. Find them." Graves hung up as he reached his SUV. It didn't surprise him that his dad had a tracker on Mom's Jeep. He was more curious about the pants reference. He really hoped Joni hadn't seen his dad bare-ass naked. Her knowing he had *one* crazy parent was bad enough. Especially when he actually had two.

He got into his SUV and hit the road, going well over the speed limit. The risk of getting a ticket from a police officer was worth it. It wouldn't be his first or last. The pack working for human law enforcement would take care of it since he was still technically out on a job.

His thoughts focused on Joni...and he found himself grinning. He wondered what she thought of his crazy mother. She wanted to be a part of his life? Well, that included dealing with his family. He'd given her plenty of opportunities to leave. Hell, he'd tried to *force* her to go.

Yeah...she kind of deserved a face-to-face with his mother.

Chapter Eleven

"I could make fried chicken. No! I'll make my famous stuffed baked chicken breasts with all the sides." Mandy beamed as she pushed the shopping cart with gusto inside the grocery store.

"Whatever's the easiest." Joni had to walk fast to keep up with the shorter woman, despite having slightly longer legs. Graves's mother was a ball of energy.

"You are such a sweet girl! We're so lucky that you're ours now."

Joni had to blink back tears. "Thank you for saying that." It was a little overwhelming, feeling so welcome after fighting with Graves to stay. Not that she'd rat him out to his mom. It would be too cruel. Mandy would probably try to spank his butt and ground him—literally. Just imagining that scenario had Joni smiling.

They hit the produce section first. "Salads are important for any dinner."

That surprised Joni. "Your…" She glanced around, watching what she said, since there were other humans around. "You eat a lot of salads? We didn't where I come from."

Mandy paused in front of the lettuce, staring at her. "No. We don't, but I just assumed your family would have fed you what other— Um, what others do." The blonde jerked her head toward an older couple shopping nearby.

Joni understood that she meant humans. "I mean, I'll eat a salad if that's what you like. But I was raised just like you," Joni assured her. "I'd toss some veggies on a plate every once in a while, because veggies are good for us in general. I love broccoli and potatoes. Mom insisted potatoes aren't that healthy, but I argued otherwise."

Mandy chuckled. "I'm guilty of that. Especially if I have chives on my baked potatoes. I mean, those are green, right? That counts." She smiled and winked at Joni. "I really do like you."

"I like you too. And I happen to love baked potatoes with chives. And cheese."

"Let's have those! Instead of stuffed chicken. What do you say about some steaks?"

"I love steak."

"That's what we'll have then." Mandy pushed away from the lettuce and headed toward the large potatoes.

Joni went for the chives. "How many are eating with us?"

"Just four, sweetie. Darlene said that my oldest son—who shall not be named, since it sounds kind of scary in public," Mandy winked at her, "will probably be gone until later tonight."

Joni couldn't pass up that opening. "Can I ask you something?"

"Anything."

"What's your son's birth name?"

Mandy turned away from the potatoes to stare at Joni.

It was instantly obvious that asking had been a mistake. "Sorry. I was just curious."

Graves's mother walked closer and lowered her voice. "It's a beautiful name...almost the same as his father's." She cleared her throat.

"He was our Angel." She paused. "But never call him that. Micah got an M name, after me. Everything changed though, and Graves stopped being that boy. He became a different man."

Joni saw the pain in those big blue eyes. "I'm so sorry."

Mandy reached out to caress her cheek. "There's nothing to be sorry about. We love Graves just the way he is. He's a good man."

"I know that."

His mother seemed to search her gaze before she smiled again, releasing her. "I see that you do. Anyway...that's his name now, and the past just contains painful memories for him. Please never call him anything else. Now, let's finish shopping or my Angelo is going to come after me. I know he activated something on my phone so he'll always know where I am. Possibly in my Jeep, too. My mate likes to think I'm unaware." She chuckled.

Joni turned, staring toward the front of the store, fully expecting Angelo to appear. He didn't.

"Don't worry. My mate is probably still searching for his keys. I hid them. He'll come, though. Angelo always worries when I go into town without him." Mandy pushed the cart toward the meat section. "He's probably called both of my sons to tattle on me. We should probably get steaks for five, after all. I'm betting that *someone* is already in his SUV, heading here as fast as possible."

Oh crap. Joni really hoped that if Graves showed up for dinner, he wouldn't be too mad. Mandy had offered to take the blame, and Joni wasn't ashamed to admit she was all for that.

"Be a sweetie and go grab a few cakes or pies for dessert from the bakery, while I hit the meat department." Mandy pointed toward the bakery area of the store. "I love chocolate anything."

"How many, exactly?"

"Get at least five of whatever you pick. Our men eat a lot."

"Got it." Joni walked away, heading toward the back of the store. The bakery was tucked in the far corner, with large ovens baking something that smelled delicious, and a single person working behind the counter. Tables and refrigerated units were scattered around the section. She checked out the pies first. Everyone liked pie. At least, *she* did.

She'd barely had time to check out the different flavors when she felt someone approaching. Joni tensed as she turned, staring up at a tall blond man.

Her instincts automatically kicked in. She'd been raised around Werewolves, so she knew one when she saw him. His large size, muscle mass, and intense stare gave it away. Some humans were that large, sure, but she just…knew.

"Easy." He had a nice voice. Deep but not a hint of snarl. "You're Joni. My name is Trent. I'm not going to hurt you. Your family hired me to find you." He stayed a few feet away, hands at his sides and his posture non-threatening. "They're worried about you."

Confusion instantly surfaced. "My parents know where I am." She'd accuse him of having the wrong person, but he clearly knew her name.

His handsome features remained calm and what she guessed was a flash of compassion filled his blue eyes. "You're off your meds, Joni. I know you probably think everything is okay, but it's not. Your brother said you get really mix up at times. You disappeared and haven't even *called* your parents. They don't know where you are."

Her confusion changed to suspicion. She didn't have a brother—what she had was an asshole who needed her to fulfill his promises to his new enforcers. "Did Brandon hire you?"

An expression of almost relief crossed the handsome Were's face. "Yes. Brandon hired me. He and your parents are worried. Will you please come with us? We'll take you to your family. They really want you to come home. I promise, you're safe now."

Joni took a step back and bumped against the refrigerator unit holding the pies and cakes. He'd said "us". She frantically looked around, instantly spotting three more large males. They hung back but their penetrating gazes were locked on her.

Four strange Weres had been sent for her.

She wasn't sure what to do. Making a scene was the ultimate no-no. It would draw attention to Weres from the humans inside the grocery store. But she wasn't about to go with them. She struggled to keep her voice from shaking.

"He's lying. Brandon is not my brother. His parents are not mine. My parents are with another pack now. My father conceded to Brandon, and he's the new pack alpha." She studied the stranger's face, glanced at the other three males, then fixed on Trent again. "You're not a part of that pack, so you wouldn't know any of this. He lied to you."

Trent kept a calm expression and showed no signs of anger. He also remained still, regarding her with his compassion-filled gaze. "Sweetheart, I know you're supposed to take medication. That you hear voices that confuse you. Brandon gave me a good rundown on what you deal with. You've got a chemical imbalance and without the meds, it messes with your reality."

"That bastard." Now Joni was seething. "I *don't* take meds. Brandon is a fucking liar." She made sure to keep her voice low. "Brandon is the asshole who just took over my old pack. He hates humans. Me, especially. He's furious that my parents sent me to another pack, where he couldn't touch me. I don't know who you are, but you've been lied to."

He seemed to study her before taking a deep breath. "How about if we go have some food and talk more? You're safe. I give my word that I won't hurt you, but until we figure this out, I won't just abandon you here alone. And I won't return you to Brandon's pack until I'm certain where you belong. My word." He paused. "But if you *are* ill, can you see how bad it would be if I just walked away? It's possible that you're confused. We're here to make sure you're safe." He glanced around before holding her gaze. "Other humans could harm you just as easily. You're an attractive, petite woman who was raised with a pack. Brandon told me his family adopted you as a young child because your birth parents abandoned you after learning of your health issues."

The tall blond clearly didn't believe her. She was also enraged that Brandon had insulted her birth parents in such an awful way. "Call Alpha Arlis. He'll clear this up. That's the pack my parents sent me to."

"Okay." He slowly reached back, withdrawing a phone from his pocket. "I'll do exactly that."

Joni felt a small measure of relief. He might not believe her but at least he was willing to make a call to verify what she'd said. "Thank you."

"No problem. All that matters is making sure you're safe." He started to tap on the screen when suddenly Joni heard a cart rushing at them.

"Get away from her!" Mandy came hauling butt, almost running with the cart and nearly hitting the blond. He had to quickly sidestep the cart to avoid a collision. Mandy got in front of Joni and growled low. "She belongs to my son. Get lost, you mangy horn dog. She's taken. Go sniff after another pretty girl."

Trent's eyes widened, and he took a step back as he inhaled deeply. It was his turn to appear confused.

"Graves is my son," Mandy softly warned. "He will tear your shit up if you even *think* about laying a finger on this girl."

Trent's shock became clear and he lowered the phone, gawking at Mandy. "You're Graves's mother? It's an honor. I'm Trent Blu." He bowed his head a little, as if in respect. "I'm no threat. We were hired for a job that I'm now deeply suspecting was false." Anger sparked in his eyes as he lifted his gaze to Joni. "You belong to Graves?"

"Yes." Joni felt the tension in her body melt away.

"Shit," he muttered. "So this Brandon who hired us..."

"Is a lying asshole," Joni supplied. "He's trying to use you to snatch me and take me back to that pack. It'll be a fate worse than death. He truly hates me."

"Son of a bitch." His gaze locked on Mandy. "I'm a friend of your son's. I had no idea. We were told Joni was mentally unwell, had wandered off after not taking her medication, and we were hired to return her to her family for her own well-being."

"That would have been the last thing you ever did!" Mandy snapped. Then she seemed to calm. "Trent Blu. My son has spoken of your pack. You're an investigator for humans and you retrieve lost pups for the packs."

"Yes." Trent returned his phone to his pocket. "And sometimes humans who packs have adopted, if they get lost. I'm sorry. We were lied to."

Mandy glanced around and sighed. "Tell your pack they can approach. You fuck with us, though, and if Graves doesn't shred you, my other son and my mate will."

Trent lifted his hand and motioned to the three other males, who approached. Two were obviously brothers with their very similar looks. The third was just scary, with parts of his head shaved and his almost black eyes. Their body posture was relaxed enough.

Mandy surprised everyone when she nodded to the third male. "You're Cable. Trent's lead enforcer." Then she motioned between the two brothers. "That makes you Reef and Kleve. Which is which?"

The slightly taller of the two arched his eyebrows. "I'm Kleve. How did you know?"

"My son tells me a lot. Mostly because I'm nosey as can be." Mandy looked over the group. "We're going to need at least five more desserts. Grab those pies or cakes and put them in the cart, Joni. We'll have to get more potatoes and steaks, too. These boys are coming to dinner." The short Were female beamed up at Trent. "That's not a request. Graves will want to talk to you about whatever moron sent you after our girl. Is this all of you or are more waiting in the parking lot?"

"It's just the four of us," Trent replied.

"Okay then. You can play guards for us and follow my Jeep home." Mandy put her hands on her hips. "You don't want Graves to have to go looking for you to get answers. He likes you. That implies I can trust you not to snatch Joni. He also said you're smart. You know he'd kill anyone, friend or not, who betrayed his mother's trust and stole his girl." Her gaze went to one of the brothers. "No flirting, kid. I've heard about you. This is one human you'd be smart not to tempt with your charms."

Trent choked a little. Joni thought he might have tried to stifle a laugh. He bowed his head again. "We'll be on our best behavior, and we'd love to join you for dinner." He shot one of the brothers a glare. "No flirting, Reef."

Mandy waved to the cart. "One of you can push that." She stepped back and to the side, hooking her arm around Joni. "Trust only goes so far. I'm sticking to her like glue. I might be small but don't let that fool you. I'm fucking mean."

Trent did laugh then. "I believe you. You birthed Graves and Micah."

"Don't you forget it." Mandy smiled up at Joni. "Have you chosen? Load up that cart."

Joni turned and started to randomly select some pies. Their group returned to the meat department, where Mandy loaded up with more steaks. They'd just reached the produce section again when she spotted Micah and his father storming toward them.

Mandy released Joni and quickly rushed forward, smiling. "It's all good. These are friends of our oldest son. They're coming to dinner."

Angelo appeared furious as he shot warning glares at the males and quickly pulled Mandy into his arms. Joni understood his protective behavior. Unfamiliar Weres were unwelcome around mated females.

Micah's reaction was the opposite. He grinned and gave Trent a back-slapping man hug. Then the other three as well. "Hey, it's great to see you. What are you doing in town?"

"Not here." Mandy elbowed her mate to get free of Angelo. "We'll talk at home." Then she quickly picked out more potatoes. "We're good to go."

Trent refused to let her pay at the checkout, using his own card to do so. Joni looked around but none of the humans seemed nervous of the six massive males. Probably due to the way Micah was talking and laughing with the one named Cable. They were discussing a football game they'd both watched, both of them animated and friendly.

They all exited the store together. Joni took the backseat of the Jeep when it became clear that Angelo wasn't leaving his mate's side. Mandy drove. A pickup containing Micah and Cable followed. Behind that was an older SUV with the other three Weres from Trent's pack.

Soon enough, they entered pack territory through the shortcut and ended up at a nice two-story home. Mandy took Joni's hand, leading her inside.

"The men can unload the groceries. Let me show you the kitchen. We'll talk while we cook."

"Sure." Joni just hoped Graves wasn't too angry when he arrived. Not only had she left his cabin, but she'd been approached by four unfamiliar

Weres and was almost returned to Brandon. It was the most eventful day she'd had in a long time.

Chapter Twelve

Graves was in a rage by the time he parked in front of his parents' home. Micah had called to give him an update—Trent and his pack had been hired to retrieve Joni. He realized they'd been lied to, and no harm had come to her, but he still wanted blood.

He rushed inside his childhood home and found everyone in the dining room. His mother sat next to Joni, with an empty chair on his human's other side. A snarl tore from his throat as he met Trent's gaze.

The male put down his silverware, his expression resigned, and slowly got to his feet. "We didn't touch Joni. Alpha Brandon said she was his mentally ill adopted sister who'd gone off her meds, and she was in danger of being hurt by humans. It's the only reason we took the job. He said she'd been raised in his pack and was clueless and too trusting. When he showed me pictures of her, it seemed clear enough that and predatory humans could target her, since she's very attractive. I swear, Graves, we just wanted to find Joni to keep her safe."

Graves looked at Joni. She was staring back, clearly nervous, but she gave him a tense smile. Her voice sounded calm when she spoke.

"They didn't touch me. Trent approached me to talk. I asked him to call Alpha Arlis, and he'd pulled out his cell to do so. That's when your mom almost ran him down with her shopping cart."

Graves shifted his attention to his mother.

Surprisingly, she actually appeared remorseful. "I'm so sorry, son. I didn't know some asshole would actually hire anyone to come after Joni.

Thankfully, it was Trent and his pack. I swear I wouldn't have taken her off territory if I'd known she was in danger, but…this *is* partially your fault for not telling me everything."

He growled loudly at his mom.

"Son," his father sighed. "You know your mother. She just wanted to spend time with Joni, so she pulled one of her stunts. The only way to stop her from doing something you know is dangerous is to explicitly explain the situation—in detail."

"He's saying this is all your fault." Micah chuckled.

Graves snarled at him next. His brother just shrugged.

"I made you a plate. It's staying warm in the microwave." His mother got up from the table and rushed into the kitchen. "I'll get you a beer. Sit next to Joni."

Graves met Trent's still tense gaze and gave him a nod, relaxing his body as he walked to the empty seat next to Joni and sat. Trent sat as well. He glanced at Reef, Kleve, and Cable. All three males watched him nervously.

"I'm not pissed at you four," Graves finally admitted. "It's *Brandon* I want to bleed."

"Thank fuck," Reef muttered. "We only took the job because we were told she was in danger. You know we're not down with women being preyed upon by any species."

Graves inclined his head as he ran a hand down Joni's jean-clad thigh. He searched her eyes when she looked at him. "Are you okay?" He inhaled, not picking up any lingering fear on her.

"I'm great." She licked her lips. "I'm sorry I left your home. Your mom…"

"Does what she wants and there's no stopping her." Graves gave her leg a gentle squeeze before addressing Trent. "Tell me what you know."

Trent explained every detail of what he'd been told. Graves accepted a beer and a plate of food from his mother. She retook her seat as all of them listened to the lies Brandon had told the other pack.

"We're supposed to call Alpha Brandon when we find his so-called sister," Trent finished.

"Tell me that you got a payment from him upfront," Graves muttered, still furious.

"Of course. We demanded a five grand deposit for our time. Some of that paid for these groceries." He smiled at Mandy. "It was the least we could do." Trent leaned back in his chair. "Brandon's an alpha, Graves. You can't just go into his territory and kill him. I know you want to, because I would feel the same way if anyone tried to take a woman under our protection."

Graves noticed that Trent hadn't called Joni his mate, but then again, the males had been close enough to scent her. They'd know that she hadn't been claimed. Just another way that Joni would remain unsafe if she wasn't with him or a member of his family at all times. "I can't let this stand. Do you know if Brandon hired anyone else?"

Cable answered. "He gave the impression he chose us because we've earned a reputation for finding and returning pups without harming them."

Trent nodded. "He also balked at paying that much for the deposit at first. I assumed either his pack's not flush with money or he's a penny pincher. So no, I don't think he hired anyone else."

Joni cleared her throat. "My father refused to give Brandon the pack's money. He set up a fifty-year trust that only the elders can access, and only once a month. It's limited in the amount they can withdraw, in order to make the money last."

Graves smirked, amused. "Limited amount?"

Joni nodded. "Enough to keep the pack afloat for at least those fifty years, if they budget expenses. It was also his way of encouraging them to continue bringing in new sources of revenue. My dad worried that Brandon would bully the elders into handing all the money over to him in one lump sum, and he'd bankrupt the pack. He's not the smartest Were in the pack...just the meanest.

"Dad also arranged for taxes on the territory to be paid automatically every year, and he put the title of all the land in the name of the trust. Brandon can't sell a single acre or take out any loans against his territory—that includes all the pack homes and businesses. At least not until the trust ends. At that point, the elders can change whatever they want. Dad figured Brandon would either learn how to become an amazing alpha, or someone would have killed him by then if he's a total fuckup. Either way, the pack is financially stable."

"I like how your father thinks." Graves was even more amused, and impressed, too.

Trent shook his head. "I'm surprised this Brandon wanted to take charge of your pack under those terms."

"Brandon didn't have a clue until after the fact," Joni admitted. "The elders swore not to tell him until the day after he became alpha, giving my mom and dad time to leave the territory. They made it safely to another pack, and I was given to Graves as a servant. We all felt it was for the best. Brandon can't retaliate against them." She sighed. "Just me, since I'm closer."

The reminder enraged Graves all over again. That fucking asshole had sent Trent's pack after Joni. He hated the idea that Brandon could have hired someone else for much less. They might have stolen her and returned her to her old pack.

"A servant?" Reef appeared shocked over that detail. "Like in the old days? For real?"

"That's not our business," Trent quickly said. "We all know Graves is a damn good guy." He gave a head nod to Graves. "However bad that sounds, we trust that it's not."

Graves liked Trent and his pack enough that he would've explained. He didn't get the chance before Joni spoke.

"I was raised with Werewolves. I'm not comfortable around humans, and I can't protect myself against many of them. My parents and I did our research, and we knew Graves would never abuse or mistreat me. We also knew his pack would have to accept me if I became his property."

She glanced around the table before she continued. Every Were at the table stared back intently. "Our elders helped to come up with that plan, actually, since modern laws aren't in favor of someone like me joining another pack. Servant or mate are the only options for a full human to be accepted. We decided not to approach Graves with a mating offer, since he'd obviously decline. I'm not worthy of someone of his status. But...one of the more ancient laws says he can't refuse a gift from a grateful pack alpha." Joni looking down at her hands. "I was gifted to him by my father. It wasn't Graves's fault. He had to accept me as his servant or risk breaching the alliance terms."

She was making excuses for him, even after the way he'd treated her when he brought her home. Guilt hit Graves—hard. "You're more than worthy to be a mate, regardless of someone's pack status."

Joni turned her head slightly to peek at him. "You would have turned the offer down flat if my father had offered me as a mate."

"But not because you're human. Because *I'm* not fit to be mated."

"Bullshit!" Micah protested.

"You would make a wonderful mate," his mom chimed in. "Tell him, Angelo."

His father met his gaze. "We raised you, Graves. You know you're caring and protective. Those are the most important qualities a good mate possesses."

"We're not discussing this," Graves stated bluntly. "Our focus should be on Brandon and the threat he poses to Joni. He needs to die."

"I agree." Trent instantly helped him change the subject. "I believed Brandon's lies because of his sincerity, and the urgency he showed in getting Joni back to his pack. He's not going to give up. Cable? What's your assessment?"

"The same. That asshole is determined to get her back," Cable grunted. "Almost frantic, actually. Which seems strange now. I mean, we mistook his strong emotions as fear and worry, because he claimed to be her adopted brother. We assumed he cared about her that much."

Reef and Kleve both nodded in agreement.

Joni said, "He wants me back to save face. He promised his unmated enforcers...certain perks. I'm sure that fear you saw was Brandon worried about losing his strongest males."

"Well, you can't just go into his territory to kill him," Trent said to Graves.

"You'll become the new alpha of his pack if you kill that asshole," Cable warned. "No offense, but you don't strike me as someone who wants that bullshit job."

Trent gave his pack mate a glare and snorted. "Says the jerk who pushed me into the role."

"Well, *you're* a sucker," Cable shot back, grinning. He tipped his head toward Graves. "Not him though. Graves, you should let us help you kill this moron, to avoid having his pack tracking you down and demanding you lead them." He looked around the table. "And I already have a plan."

He nodded. "I'm listening. Technically, as a judge, I can't break the laws, even if I really want to. But I'm going to take him out regardless. He's left me with no other choice by coming after Joni. I'd just prefer to keep it all legal."

"That's my son." Mandy proudly beamed.

"The trick will be getting him out of his territory and into ours," Cable explained. "Then it's not seen as an alpha challenge. He won't be stupid enough to step foot in *your* territory."

"Exactly what I'm thinking," Trent mused. "I'll tell him that I retrieved Joni but learned the truth of who she is to you. Make sure he knows I'm furious that he risked bringing down the wrath of Alpha Arlis's pack on mine and refuse to travel to his pack. He'll have to come to us if he wants to collect her."

"You're not taking my daughter!" Mandy stood, growling again. "She's not bait."

"Mom, sit," Graves ordered. "Joni will be safe. She'll remain at my place."

"I don't mind being bait," she offered. "It's probably better if I'm there so Brandon can see me. Otherwise, he might just take off. You can't fight him if he just drives away."

Graves frowned at her, but she refused to back down.

"Brandon isn't going to stop, Graves. And I know you won't let anything happen to me. Not to mention...I'm human. That means I can defend myself with a gun, right? My parents taught me how to shoot. Arm me. I'll shoot Brandon or any of his enforcers if they reach me during the fight."

Graves had to admire her courage, even if he didn't like her idea. "It's legal, if a human living with a pack shoots an aggressive Were in self-defense," he reluctantly admitted.

"Graves!" his mother hissed.

He turned to her. "This new alpha needs to be dealt with, and I refuse to take control of some fucking pack just to kill him. You know what I do, Mom. Trust me. No one is taking Joni from us. And we're just discussing options."

His mother clearly wasn't convinced. "Fine. *You* discuss. *I'm* taking Joni to my craft room."

Joni hesitated. Graves knew she wanted to be part of this discussion. He patted her leg. "I'll share what we come up with later. Go with my mom."

She didn't look happy, but surprisingly, Joni rose from her seat and followed his mom out of the dining room.

Once he figured they were far enough out of hearing range, Graves gave his full attention to Trent and Cable. "I don't want to drag your pack into this mess. There's only six of you. No offense, but the last thing you need with those low numbers is a fight on your doorstep."

All four of them immediately tensed at his words. It caused him to smile as he held Trent's gaze. "I've known about Jay since I first investigated your pack for my alpha. I didn't share anything about him. It actually made me respect you even more, once I realized why you'd lied to me by saying there were only five males in your pack. The fact that you'd protect him at the expense of your own safety impressed the hell out of me, Trent."

Micah cleared his throat. "Is this Jay wanted by another pack for bullshit crimes or something?"

Graves looked at his brother. "You're not here and you never heard any of this." He shifted his gaze to their father. "You either."

His father gave a nod of confirmation. "You can count on me being deaf and having a shit memory. You know I never repeat anything you say to me in confidence."

When they pointedly stared at Micah, he looked back and forth between them. "Hey, *I'm* not going to blab. But what supposed crime did he commit? Now I'm imagining the worst."

Graves glanced at Trent. It was his call.

Trent stared back, one brow raised.

Graves took a deep breath. "I told you about my cousin Wen. We're cool with VampLycans and GarLycans. They aren't going to give a shit or tell anyone."

"You have one of them living with you?" Micah grinned. "Holy shit! I didn't think any of them would integrate into a pack?"

"Go ahead," Cable muttered. "I trust the blood kin of Graves."

Reef and Kleve both nodded.

Trent glanced between Micah and his father. "Jay *is* a shifter...but he's not what you're thinking. Let's just say we're damn grateful he doesn't cough up furballs."

Graves couldn't help but grin as he watched those words sink in as his father and brother realized the truth. It was his father who spoke first.

"*Fuck*. Are you messing with us? I didn't think any feline shifters existed in the US anymore. He's got to be one badass motherfucker to have survived. What an asset to your pack."

"A cat shifter?" Micah whispered, eyes wide in shock. "For real? I've got to meet him! That is so fucking cool! I totally want to become his bestie."

Trent and his pack relaxed. Cable grinned and shook his head at Micah.

"I told you," Graves said before shooting his brother a smirk. "And Jay has way better taste than making you his best friend. I mean, he hangs with these guys. They're cooler than you could *ever* be."

Everyone laughed, including Micah.

Trent grew serious as he finally replied to Graves. "We can handle a little trouble when it's this kind. And you're not dragging us into anything. Alpha Brandon dragged us into this mess when he decided to lie and hire us to grab Joni. We're not going to stand for some prick using us to help him hurt a woman. What the fuck is this asshole's problem?"

Graves shared what Joni had told him about Brandon and his plans to turn her into a pack whore for his enforcers.

"He needs to die!" Trent snarled.

"I'm in on whatever goes down," Micah growled. "I want to kill these assholes."

"Me too," their father stated.

Graves met his dad's gaze. "Your job is to stay here and protect Mom."

"Maybe knock her up," Micah suggested with a grin. "She's baby crazy. Give her another one is the best thing you could do, Dad."

Graves couldn't exactly argue with his younger brother's assessment. Their mother *did* need something to occupy her time. Having another baby might keep her busy enough to stop interfering in his life. "I don't even want to think about you doing that, but I agree. Joni wouldn't have been taken into town if Mom wasn't so desperate for a daughter. Give her a few more pups. Maybe you'll get a girl next time."

"She's set on having grandpups." Their dad glanced between them.

"Tough shit," Micah muttered. "I'm not mating anytime soon, and Graves is a stubborn jerk. Tag, you're it, Dad. Knock her up."

Reef laughed. "I love this family."

Cable leaned forward, getting them back on track. "I hate to say this, but I agree with Joni. Our chances of luring this alpha into our territory are better if we have your female, Graves. The asshole might want proof she's with us."

"Agreed." Trent reluctantly nodded.

"I'm thinking the land we bought last month is a great spot for an ambush." Cable glanced at his pack mates.

Trent nodded again, but he focused on Graves when he responded. "A human neighbor sold us just over a hundred acres in a heavily wooded area that adjoins our current territory. I'll say that's where we're keeping her. There's a small cabin on the property, but most of the dirt road leading to it got washed out years ago from storms. Even off-road vehicles can't traverse it to reach the cabin now. Too much vegetation. They'll barely be able to see it from where they'd have to park, and they'd definitely have to walk in the rest of the way."

"I wouldn't even call it a cabin anymore," Kleve said. "It's rotted inside and a portion of the roof collapsed, but you can't see the damage from the road. It's on the backside. We can claim we didn't want her in our territory after we learned who she belongs to; let's face it, you're terrifying, Graves." He grinned at him. "And no one know we're the owners of that land since it's a recent purchase."

"But we won't really have her inside it, of course," Trent added. "I wouldn't risk the rest of that cabin not falling down. We'll just hide her behind it and bring her out 'the back door,'" he air-quoted, "if they want proof that she's with us."

"I'll be her guard," Micah said. He glanced at Trent's males. "Does this dick who hired you know all the males in your pack?"

Trent shook his head. "Only the four of us were in the office when they came to hire my pack. Alpha Brandon did ask if we were the only members. I told him we handle the office work, while the rest hunt whoever we're paid to find. I like to give strangers the impression that we have more numbers than we actually do, whenever possible."

"That's smart." Micah licked his lips, looking excited. "I'll pose as a member of your pack and take down anyone who gets past you guys, before they can lay a claw on Joni." He looked at Graves, his expression serious. "You can trust me to keep her safe."

Graves had no doubt. His younger brother was normally good-natured and friendly, but they'd grown up sparring together. Micah had a brutal side when warranted. "I trust you with Joni's safety."

Micah smiled.

Trent didn't. "We'll have Jay there, too, but he'll stay out of sight unless he's needed. Weres never expect to be attacked from above."

"I can't wait to meet this badass!" Micah sounded downright gleeful.

Graves resisted rolling his eyes. "When do you want this to go down?"

Trent hesitated, obviously thinking. "As soon as possible. Alpha Brandon knows we're renowned for finding our targets quickly. I'll call him tonight and arrange the meeting for first thing in the morning. It would be nice if he showed up while it's still dark, but he didn't seem like a *total* moron. He'll want to be in unknown territory during the day. I'll tell him to meet us at eight, but I'm guessing he'll come at dawn to surprise us."

"Maybe we should let this asshole stew for a few days, until he's more desperate. To make sure he'll come pick up Joni himself," Micah muttered.

Graves shook his head. "Brandon is already desperate, since he paid someone money he doesn't have to come after something who belongs to *me*. He's not ignorant of my reputation."

"I'm surprised his asshole even thought it was possible for us to obtain Joni, if he knew she was with you," Trent admitted. "We didn't expect her to be with a pack. He told us to search the nearby towns."

"Joni did the grocery shopping and cooking for their pack house," Graves explained, "and her parents always sent enforcers to protect her around humans. So this Brandon probably figured we'd give her the same job, but wouldn't value her enough to afford her the same protection."

"So basically we got lucky," Kleve mused. "We only found her because your mother took Joni shopping."

Graves nodded.

Reef took a drink of beer before shaking his head. "This alpha is a total moron to fuck with you, Graves." He smirked at Micah. "Do you have any idea what kind of reputation your brother has? He's a living, breathing nightmare to shitty Weres."

Trent growled low. "That fucker set us up in more ways than we thought. Alpha Brandon is relying on some obscure pack laws to get away with this shit. I should know; I had to study them carefully when we decided to claim territory and send notices of our intent to all the surrounding packs within two hundred miles of us."

"I don't get it What laws are you talking about?" Reef asked.

Graves was the one who explained. "To put it in simple terms, Joni is considered property, since she was gifted to me. I can only punish anyone who steals her *directly* from me. That means, by law, punishment would fall on the four of you, if you'd snatched Joni from that grocery store. Any third party you might give my property to is in the clear.

"Essentially, Brandon could claim he'd accepted Joni in good faith from your pack, and remain legally clear of repercussions. Imagine what would have happened if I'd shown up, looking to get her back, but you'd already handed her off to those assholes."

Cable snarled. "Fuck! You could have wiped us out—and been justified in doing it."

Graves nodded. "When Trent calls him, I'm guessing Brandon will depend on me killing you. Maybe even your entire pack, leaving no survivors who might go after him in retaliation for tricking you into stealing from me. Which I would have done...if we weren't friends and I didn't trust you."

"Thank fuck for that," Kleve grumbled.

Reef leaned forward. "Then how are you going to legally kill this motherfucker, if those are the laws?"

"There are loopholes in every law, if you look hard enough." Graves held Trent's gaze. "Do you want to explain or should I?"

Trent didn't hesitate. "Graves can't breach Alpha Brandon's territory to retrieve Joni, since they didn't technically take her. But *anyone* in our territory is fair game—including Brandon, if he arrives himself to claim her."

"Brandon is going to die by my claws." Graves fisted his hands on the table. "No one else is allowed to take him down. He's *mine*."

He and Trent stared at each other for long seconds.

The other male gave a nod, conceding. "Joni is your female. We won't touch him, despite what he tried to do to us. Make the prick suffer, though."

"I have a question. Can you take over this prick's pack if he dies in your territory, Trent?" Micah sipped his beer. "That's one way to majorly increase your numbers."

"Fuck that," Trent answered. "And no. I'd have to fight him inside his territory after issuing a challenge to officially win control of his pack. I don't want more on my plate." He glanced at Graves. "Alpha Brandon is all yours. We're just letting you use our territory to engage him, and we'll have your back, since he brought three enforcers with him last time. We'll handle them."

"Dibs," Reef and Kleve said at the same time.

Graves leaned back in his chair and nodded. "We'll leave well before sunrise to get set up in your territory. I want this threat to Joni annihilated as soon as possible."

Chapter Thirteen

Joni sat quietly in the backseat, listening in as Graves and Micah spoke softly in the front of the SUV. It was four in the morning, and they were following the other pack into their territory. She felt nervous and worried. Her trust in Graves was absolute. Despite liking Trent and his males, she wasn't certain if her faith in them was equally justified.

All the things that could go wrong cycled through her head. Brandon could have Trent's pack secretly working for him. Graves did have a habit of making a lot of enemies, thanks to his job.

She was just grateful that he'd allowed her to come. So much so that she hesitated to voice her concerns.

"Is she always this quiet?" Micah twisted in the seat to peer back at Joni.

She couldn't make out his face well, since it was pitch black outside. The dash inside the vehicle didn't put off much light.

"No," Graves responded. "I won't let anything happen to you, Joni. Have you changed your mind about acting as bait? I can turn around and drive you back to my place. Micah can stay in one of my guest rooms until this is over, to make sure you're safe."

If she wanted to speak up, the time was now. "No. I need to be there, just in case Brandon demands to see me. But...are you sure we can trust Trent's pack? They could betray you. I'll assume that most of them aren't mated. That they need access to females. Brandon would promise anything to gain their loyalty. Maybe he offered them introductions."

Graves chuckled. "I see where you're going with this, but I *do* trust Trent and his pack. They aren't the types to screw over allies, whether they have mates or not. I know for a fact that one of them, at least, has no problems gaining access to unmated bitches. Cable has more than enough willing sex partners from at least two packs that I'm aware of. Three, if you count the fact that he hooked up with a woman from *our* pack not too long ago. Arlis has no rules about sexual hookups with other packs, as long as they do it off territory.

"None of Trent's other males have ever asked me to introduce them to our unmated females, but if any of them did, I'd gladly set it up. They're damn good people. Any women they take into their pack would be treated well."

That lessened some of her uneasiness. "Okay. What's their motive then? They're basically allowing you to take over their territory while this goes down. Alphas don't do that. It's against their nature."

"Between the three of us? Trent and his males are grateful to me, despite my telling them repeatedly that there's no debt owed."

"Why? What do they owe you for?" Micah asked the questions before Joni could.

"I was sent to investigate them when they claimed their territory and notified the nearby alphas of their new pack. They were braced for the worst. And I could have been an asshole about it. I wasn't. I prefer to be fair, and I treated them accordingly. Trent and his males earned my respect, and I assured the other alphas that they weren't a threat. Since then, Trent's pack has officially been accepted as allies." Graves paused. "I honestly believe Trent expected me to chase them out. It's sad, but it happens to newly formed packs often. Anyway, that's why they feel beholden. None of those males will screw me over. I'd even consider them good friends."

"Okay." Joni finally relaxed. "Are you really going to kill Brandon?"

"Yes. Do you have a problem with that?"

She inwardly flinched at his snarling tone. "No. Brandon brought this on himself. I just feel bad for his family. His parents and sister will grieve his loss. They love him, but they understand that he's flawed. It's just…" *Heartbreaking.* She didn't want to say that aloud though.

"He came after you, and he betrayed a good pack to take the fall for his crime, Joni. There's no forgiving that. Do you think my beating him to near death but allowing him to return to his pack will stop him from trying to get to you in the future? Will it make him a better alpha who won't fuck over others? Be honest."

She couldn't lie to Graves. "No. He'll be shamed if he returns to the pack after losing a fight and will want revenge. On me, you, your pack, *and* Trent's."

"One of the first things I learned is that feeling pity for family members shouldn't influence justice." Graves paused. "Brandon will harm others in the same shitty way or worse if I don't stop him now. Then all his future bad actions will fall on me, because I allowed him to live. Think of the suffering we're preventing. That's what I focus on."

"Listen to my brother," Micah added. "He's right. It sucks for family members, losing someone they love, but this Brandon gave no shits about the deadly consequences that Trent and his pack would suffer if they'd successfully grabbed you. He also didn't consider any of the repercussion for his family or his pack, if things went bad." He studied her over his shoulder. "And what if it hadn't been Trent who came after you? Not all trackers are respectable. You might have been killed...and don't forget that our mother was with you. They could have taken or murdered her, too."

He turned around, shaking his head. "Someone who hires strangers to kidnap others, especially if they're women or kids, shouldn't be breathing. If this asshole alpha is capable of that, he's also capable of a lot worse."

"You're both right," she admitted quietly. "Sorry."

"Don't apologize," Graves said. "You have a kind heart, Joni. Unfortunately, Brandon doesn't. I'm going to keep you safe. That means taking out the threat."

"Thank you." Joni hugged her chest.

"And don't thank me, either," he rasped. "It's my job. You're mine now."

Micah turned in the seat yet again, grinning at her this time. "You heard him. You're his, Joni."

"Shut up," Graves growled.

Micah laughed. Then he changed the subject. "So...do you think Dad will actually knock up Mom up again? She's been attempting to set me up with every unmated female she knows. Last week, she tried to talk me into having dinner with Kendra."

Graves burst into a full-on belly laugh.

"Bro, that's not funny. I'd rather ask a hungry Vamp to give me a blow job than spend a minute with Kendra or her two idiot best friends. And that's saying *everything* when someone biting my dick sounds better."

Joni was glad both men were facing forward, since her mouth dropped open. She couldn't resist asking a question. "Who's Kendra?"

Micah twisted in his seat for a fourth time. "She and her two best friends are the worst members in our pack. Seriously. They're idiotically vain, dumb as bricks, and just plain mean." He shook his head. "I mean, have you ever met any Weres who actually got boob jobs? You will if you run into those three."

That stunned her even more. "What happens to their breast implants when they shift into fur?"

"Nothing good." Micah snorted. "They somehow found a way around that little healing ability of ours to expel foreign objects from our bodies, but imagine wolves with two huge lumps hanging from their undersides."

Graves laughed even harder. "They're one of the many reasons I don't show up when Arlis arranges pack runs to help the unmated find hookups. I don't *ever* want to see that."

"Those three bitches would piss themselves if you did. I'm sure they're just as terrified of you as everyone else. Even they aren't stupid enough to believe that you'd put up with their narcissistic bullshit." Micah laughed with his brother.

"True enough," Graves agreed. He grew somber. "We're almost to Trent's territory. Be on alert. I don't trust Brandon not to have someone watching their pack. This asshole had to pay them five grand upfront. It implies Brandon will owe even more after the job is finished."

That seemed to dull Micah's humor. "Do you think these fuckers were planning on attacking Trent's pack to take Joni by force, so they don't have to pay the rest?"

"No—I think it's possible that they planned to outright slaughter them. Trent and Cable will have realized the same." Graves snarled. "I don't want to think about what would've happened if they'd stolen Joni, then I showed up to find them dead."

"What do you mean?" Joni asked.

Graves stared at her intently in the rearview. "I wouldn't know for certain why they took you or where you'd gone. Though, given what you've told me, I would've suspected Brandon and your old pack of being behind it."

"I really am starting to hate this guy," Micah sighed. "Thanks for letting me come with."

"Just don't hold back." Graves deepened his voice. "You tend to avoid making kills. They deserve more than just having their asses handed to them if they get close to Joni. Take them the fuck out."

"Believe me, I plan to." Micah nodded. "These aren't just annoying pack members who've earned a beat down. I won't hesitate to kill, Graves."

Guilt twisted inside Joni that he even had to consider doing so for her. "I'm so sorry."

"You aren't responsible for any of this," Grave firmly reminded her. "Are you sure you want to be here to see what happens when Brandon arrives? It's going to be brutal."

"I was raised as an alpha's daughter. I might be human, but I don't think like one." She looked out the window beside her. "And I'm apologizing because my baggage has affected you both. I really believed that at most, Brandon would just ask Arlis to return me to him. I didn't think he was foolish enough to pull this kind of stunt."

"You did nothing to deserve any of this," he assured her. "Now get down, Joni. We're almost there. Even a Were shouldn't be able to see us with the tint on my windows, but I'm not taking any chances. If those assholes are here, they'll probably attack the moment they spot you."

She undid her seat belt and moved to sit on the floor. "Are you going to give me a gun? I can handle handguns, rifles, and shotguns. My aim is pretty great, if I say so myself."

"Hot," Micah loudly whispered. "That's a good skill for a mate to have."

"Shut it," Graves snapped. "Reach under Micah's seat carefully. There's a .22 tucked inside a leather holster. There's also an extra clip. It's loaded but the safety is on."

Her eyebrows shot up and she stuck her hand under the passenger seat, feeling around. She found the gun quickly, as well as the clip tucked above it.

"You keep weapons under the seats? What if you're pulled over by human police?"

Joni wondered about that too. She was glad Micah had brought it up.

"I have permits to carry concealed weapons in the glovebox. I'm a licensed bodyguard and private detective, according to human laws. The legally registered weapons are under the front seats and in the trunk area. I also have hidden compartments in the back, under the dash, and on the underside of my vehicle, for weapons that aren't registered."

"Fuck." Micah sounded impressed. "I had no idea you owned that many guns."

"A lot of rogues don't use claws or fangs to fight me. Sometimes I'm outnumbered when I come across crazy Vamps, too. The firepower comes in handy. Blowing big holes into their bodies at least slows them down and evens the odds. I've got body armor too." Graves nodded toward the windshield. "The dirt road ahead is going to be rough. Grab hold of something. And Joni, keep the safety on that gun until you get out of the SUV or we're attacked. I don't want it accidently going off."

"Got it." She blindly felt the gun. It was a small handgun. The bullets would only irritate a Were, even if she unloaded an entire clip into one. "I really need a shotgun."

Graves shook his head. "You won't be able to tell if we're friend or foe when we're all shifted, since you've never seen any of us in fur. Especially if it's dark. Your eyesight and sense of smell aren't as keen as ours. So don't even use that gun unless a wolf leaps at you. No, it won't kill them, but it'll fucking hurt and give Micah time to take them out. The only thing in fur you'll be able to trust for certain is a cougar. He's one of Trent's. *Don't* shoot Jay."

Joni was too stunned to speak. *A cougar?* She'd heard about cat shifters, but they were basically just rumors and legends. She was grateful that Graves told her about the feline in Trent's pack.

There were a lot Weres in her old pack that she could identify in fur, but not all. Some looked a lot alike, unless they had special markings or distinct colors.

"I understand," she belatedly answered.

"What do you aim for if anyone comes at you?"

Joni didn't have to think about the answer. "Eyes, into an open mouth, and, if it's at close range, upper part of the throat."

"Excellent," Graves approved. "Your pack taught you well."

"I thought it would be the heart and lungs," Micah said.

Graves snorted. "Wrong. But you weren't trained to fight Weres with guns. We have thicker bones than humans, so our heart and lungs are well-protected. And with the weapon I gave her, you need to hit softer targets. Any mouth damage will cause a Were to choke, or even cut off their airway if the throat fills with blood. They'll heal, but they'll be down for a short while. Eyes are hard to hit, but if you do...worst case, you blinded them in at least one eye, which throws off their balance off. Best case, that can also take them down for a while. Both are effective ways to buy some time in a fight."

"Our escorts are slowing down." Micah unfastened his seat belt. "We're here. Are we checking out the area first before Joni gets off the floor?"

"Yes." Graves stopped the SUV and killed the engine. "Stay down, Joni. I'm leaving the keys right here but locking the doors. Take off if shit hits the fan. Return to my pack and go directly to the alpha's office."

"Okay," she softly agreed…but she was lying.

There was no way she'd drive off and leave Graves and his brother behind. Not only had she learned how to fight and use guns, but one of the enforcers had spent significant time teaching her defensive driving. The SUV itself could be turned into a weapon.

Plowing a heavy vehicle into a Were or driving over one would do a lot more damage than the sad little handgun she'd been given.

* * * * *

Graves grabbed the second fob for his SUV that he kept hidden under the dash and slid out of the vehicle. He waited until his brother had exited before locking the doors. His gaze took in the heavily wooded area. Trent's two vehicles had stopped ahead of him, where the dirt road ended. He inhaled, not picking up any scents that shouldn't be there.

Trent walked back to him. "The cabin is a quarter of a mile to the north. We'll have Alpha Brandon come in from another other road. This is basically a back way. I didn't want him to see our vehicles in case he can identify yours."

"Smart." Graves kept his gaze roaming and his senses on high alert. He heard a slight crack sound and tensed, ready to shift and attack.

"Easy," Trent murmured. "It's Jay. He's been scouting the area. I told him to make a little noise as he came in to make sure he didn't startle anyone."

Graves instantly looked up into the surrounding trees. A dark shape leapt toward them from high above. There was only a slight thump as the huge cougar landed on the ground, fifty feet away. It slowly stalked closer.

"Badass," Micah whispered. "Look at the size of you! No wonder you've survived."

Cable approached the cougar shifter and crouched, talking low. "Anything out there?"

The cougar used one massive front paw and began tapping the ground. Graves couldn't see what it wrote or indicated, since Cable partially blocked his view.

"Got it." Cable stood and turned. "One scout was left near Logan Road. That's where we lost them yesterday, when the bastards attempted to follow us back to our packhouse after hiring us. No one has encroached beyond that." He turned, addressing the cat. "In a vehicle?"

The cougar shook his big head, batted his paw in the air, and growled.

Trent translated, "The scout is patrolling in fur by the road, probably waiting for us to leave our territory. Clearly they think we're amateurs, leaving ourselves only one way in or out."

"*Badass*," Micah whispered again.

"Shut up," Graves ordered his brother.

"Jay, this is Graves." Trent motioned to him. "And his younger brother, Micah. The woman, Joni, is in the SUV. Relax. We're all friends here."

Graves studied the large cougar. There was no mistaking it was a shifter, with his sheer size and muscle mass. Jay stayed back from him and his brother, obviously leery as hell of anyone not from his own pack. Not that he blamed him. Packs had hunted feline shifters into extinction in the states. The fact that Jay had survived at all was impressive as hell.

"We have no issue with you, Jay. The moment I found out about you, I respected your pack even more. We have no problem with *any* shifters. We're actually related to VampLycans."

"Can I pet you?"

Graves wanted to smack his brother. "God, Micah! You sound like a pup."

"What? He is so fucking cool!"

Jay made a soft chattering noise and slowly advanced. Graves tensed but held utterly still. The cougar walked up to Micah, pausing a foot away as the two studied each other.

His brother grinned. "You're fucking amazing! Your eyes are way cool too, dude. Seriously."

Jay gave a soft snort and turned, paused, then side-stepped closer and lightly bumped into Micah's jean-clad thigh.

His bother didn't hesitate to lightly run his hand over the large shifter's back.

The cougar put up with being petted for about ten seconds before strutting away, his tail whipping around. He moved between Reef and Kleve, softly growling.

"Go ahead," Trent replied. "We're right behind you."

Jay suddenly took off, rushed toward a tree, and leapt. He was out of sight in seconds, lost in the thick branches.

"I want to be a cat shifter."

Graves rolled his eyes. "We're here for a reason, and it's not for you to go all fanboy on poor Jay. Grow the fuck up."

"Killjoy," Micah muttered.

Graves unlocked the SUV and opened the back door, offering his hand to Joni. "It's safe. Let's go. We're walking to the cabin. Can you see anything?"

"Not much," she admitted. "In the woods and before sunrise? It's pretty dark."

Graves put his arm around Joni's waist to keep her from tripping on the uneven ground, due to her human eyesight.

After several steps, he pulled her closer. *Protective measure. Nothing more.*

Chapter Fourteen

Joni wished she had enhanced shifter vision. The moon was full but the woods were dense with trees. Their branches blocked out most of the faint light. She'd have probably tripped dozens of times if it wasn't for Graves hugging her against his side. His strong arm kept her steady. He'd even just picked her up a few times to carry her over fallen logs or other large objects in their path.

"We're here," Graves softly rasped close to her ear.

Joni spotted a clearing ahead. She was able to make out more without the heavy tree cover. A dilapidated shack sat near the back of the open area. It reminded her of something she'd see in a horror movie.

It was hard to make out the details, but she could see enough to tell that it wasn't livable and hadn't been in a very long time. The roofline sagged in a few places, as if years of storms had worn it down. The inside was probably one rotted mess, full of nests of any creepy crawlers found in the area. She really hoped she wouldn't have to actually go inside.

"I just got a text." Trent's voice startled her. "The bastard says he'll be here at eight in the morning to pick her up and pay the rest of the money."

Someone, one of Trent's males, made a disbelieving snort. The noise startled Joni.

Graves pulled her tighter against his side. "Easy," he whispered.

Someone tall approached. "Jay will warn us if any of those assholes try to sneak up on us." It turned out to be Cable, speaking low. "He's up high in the trees and can see the surrounding area. He can spot a mouse almost a mile away. Cats *do* love chasing rodents."

There was a soft cracking sound, as if a thin branch snapped.

Cable laughed. "His hearing is damn good too. No offense, Jay," he said a little louder, talking in the direction of the noise. He moved closer to Graves. "We had Parker bring some supplies for your Joni."

"He's here too?" Graves asked, looking around.

"No. He's back at the packhouse, watching the surveillance feeds that cover our territory." Cable looked at Joni. "He's our computer expert. We keep him out of fights, but Trent had him bring a few things out here earlier, with Jay watching over him to make sure it was safe."

"Is he that unstable?" Joni had to strain to hear the words from Graves.

"He carries some scars," Cable replied. "I'd trust Parker to have my back in a fight any time, but we promised Brandon was yours. Unleashing Parker...well, let's just say he can tell friend from foe, but he's got no off switch once blood is spilled until every threat is in a lot of pieces."

"Got it."

Joni shivered against Graves. Unlike him, she *didn't* get it. Parker sounded extremely dangerous. It made her glad he wasn't anywhere near her.

"Let's get your woman settled." Cable started to walk toward the shack.

Graves kept her at his side, his arm a steel manacle around her shoulders. Joni cleared her throat. "Please tell me I'm not going inside. I don't want to meet whatever animals have made that dump home."

A soft chuckle came from Cable. "No. It's not safe inside. The roof is mostly collapsed along the back already. Parker left you a sleeping bag and a pillow. You should rest while you can and try to stay warm."

So that's how Joni ended up curled inside a thick sleeping bag with a comfy pillow. An hour later, she still hadn't slept. Graves sat a few feet away. Cable stayed with him, also keeping low to the ground.

"No one coming in from that road will see us here," he promised. "This side is rotted to hell, but the front logs are sturdy enough to protect her from bullet spray if those assholes have no honor and bring human weapons."

Joni wished she could deny that Brandon and his enforcers wouldn't break pack laws by showing up with guns, but she couldn't, so she stayed silent. She'd never thought he'd hire someone to kidnap her, either. Brandon was obviously desperate to fulfill his promise to his enforcers.

Cable whispered, "Trent just motioned to me that Parker spotted movement on the west end of the property. Those assholes have definitely come early in an attempt to take us out."

"Did you realize they probably planned to slaughter your entire pack?"

Joni shivered at how cold and emotionless Graves sounded when he asked that question.

"It crossed our minds. This asshole alpha really is a dumbass if he believes you wouldn't automatically know who'd hire us to take your woman."

"I have no faith that he's intelligent at all."

Joni couldn't disagree with Graves's assessment. Brandon had proven that he was a moron. Every Werewolf knew never to mess with a judge. Especially Graves. "Are they going to attack us soon?" She kept her voice low.

"We figured around dawn," Cable said. "You probably can't see Trent's hand signals. They breached our territory on the far west side and are moving in slowly." He softly chuckled. "Probably thinking they're sneaking up on us. Jay will watch over them until they get close. We'll know before they spring their attack."

Joni felt a little better. Both for Jay's protection, and for the fact the sun wouldn't come up for another hour.

Graves approached her and crouched, putting his lips near her ear. "When the time comes, pretend that Micah is your captor. Act scared, use me as a threat… I want those bastards to think they aren't walking into a trap. Just keep yelling loudly as they approach. Do you understand?"

She did. It would prove she was there, and Brandon would keep coming instead of turning tail to flee for his life. "Yes."

"It'll be over soon. I need to be in the woods before they get a better view of the clearing. Do everything that Micah tells you when the attack happens. And don't shoot anyone unless they try to lunge at you."

Joni nodded.

Graves reached out to gently caress the side of her face. "I hate to leave you, but I don't want Brandon running away if he sees me. I doubt he could win in a race between us, but he might have some nasty surprises waiting out of Trent's territory that they can't see. Like half a dozen armed Weres ready to shoot me."

She didn't need him to explain that enough bullets could kill a Werewolf. "Be careful." She had a fierce urge to kiss him, to know what it felt like just once, in case anything happened. But she didn't think he'd appreciate it.

He stroked her cheek again. "Remain quiet until Micah gives you the word, then get loud. Argue, plead, and threaten. Sell it."

"I can do that. I swear." Joni knew their lives depended on it.

Graves released Joni and straightened, walking toward his brother. The further away from the woman he got, the tenser he became.

He probably should have told her sooner that he wanted her to raise a little hell to make sure Brandon stayed in the area. He just didn't want to worry her, or have too much time to stew about before the attack.

Micah met him in the woods. "I know the plan and can totally pretend to be an asshole. Don't get killed. I'll protect Joni. Mom would never forgive me if anything happened to my new sister."

Graves glared. It was another dig at him to mate Joni.

"Hey, you heard Mom. Joni's her daughter." His brother smirked, not even pretending to be innocent, despite his amended words.

Micah slapped him on the shoulder and left to keep Joni company. When Cable joined him in the woods, the both headed in the direction the enemy would arrive from.

Dozens of yards into the woods, Graves found a thick tree to lean against, keeping very still. Cable did the same nearby. Time passed slowly. No one spoke, and he kept his gaze trained on the surrounding woods.

When Trent finally motioned to them that the enemy was near, it didn't take long for Graves to spot their movement in the distance. He counted seven males in human form, rushing from tree to tree, trying to stay out of sight. He resisted rolling his eyes.

The sky started to lighten quickly as dawn approached.

Cable used his hand to signal that he was going to circle behind the approaching males. For such a large guy, he kept low and didn't make a sound. It impressed Graves. He instantly decided that if he ever needed backup on a job, he'd ask Trent and his pack if they wanted to earn some extra money.

"Stop fighting me, you little bitch!"

The unexpected shout from Micah startled Graves so much, he whipped his head toward the dilapidated cabin. Trent must have signaled to his brother.

"He's gonna hunt you down and rip you to pieces, you spineless prick!" Joni yelled back. "You'll die for this. I belong to Graves!"

"Shut up," Micah growled. "Please tell me I can hit her, Alpha. She's giving me a goddamn headache. This fucking human is annoying as hell!"

"No," Trent snarled. "Just remember the money we're getting and suck it up."

"You're dead too, you asshole," Joni practically screamed. "Graves will find out who kidnapped me. He'll come for you!" She paused. "Just take me back!"

"Shut the fuck up," Micah bellowed. "Come on. Let me hurt her just a little. God, I can't believe anyone would pay for this mouthy bitch."

"Enough!" Trent ordered. "She's just off her meds. I promised we'd hand her over unharmed. Her brother will get here in a couple hours, pay us, and we'll have a drink to celebrate."

Graves let his claws slide out as he prepared to fight the incoming Weres. It infuriated him that he'd had to put Joni in danger because of what Brandon had done. He couldn't wait to tear into the fucker. It was rare that he actually enjoyed killing, but the situation wasn't normal—it was personal.

"Fine," Micah barked. "Shut up, crazy pants."

"Fuck you! I'm not insane. You're being lied to! Graves is going to kill you all!"

"You *are* annoying. Shut it," Trent snarled. "Jesus, I hope you're not like this when you're back on your meds. Your brother is a fucking saint. *I* sure as hell wouldn't put up with you."

Graves was impressed with how well they were playing their roles. There was no doubt the Brandon and his men could hear everything being said in the clearing.

He spotted more movement. Brandon and his enforcers were moving faster, probably feeling overconfident that the arguing would not only cover the sound of their approach, but that Trent and his males would be too distracted to put up much of a fight. He was grateful the morning breeze kept him downwind of the enemy.

When Brandon and his enforcers finally reached the edge of the clearing, Trent suddenly snarled, facing the direction they'd come from. "Come out. I smell you!"

A tall blond strode out of the tree line with a friendly smile on his face. "Sorry I'm early. I was too worried about my sister to wait."

"Fuck you, Brandon! You're not going to get away with this," Joni warned. "Graves is going to rip you to shreds for talking these idiots into kidnapping me."

The blond's expression turned almost smug as he glared at Joni. "I told you to take your meds, sis. We're going back home and I'll take good care of you. I'll make sure you never run away again."

Graves bristled at the thinly veiled threat, but waited to attack. That would change in an instant if Brandon went after Joni. No way would he allow that asshole to get within striking distance of her.

"You can have the rest of your enforcers step out. You brought the cash, right?" Trent took a step closer Brandon. "This is a simple deal. No need to be wary of each other. We're both respectable men."

"Of course." Brandon tore his glare off Joni, glancing around the clearing. "Where are the rest of your males?"

"At home," Trent lied. "I didn't need more than one of mine to handle your sister while we completed our transaction. I'm ready to make the trade."

Six of Brandon's enforcers stepped into the clearing, flanking their alpha. They all wore black from throat to feet. It not only helped them remain camouflaged at night, but blood would be harder to spot on their clothing and boots. It just cemented his suspicion that Brandon had no plans to pay Trent. Their intent was to slaughter the small pack.

"Come here, Joni." Brandon her forward with a hand.

"Fuck. *You.*" Joni didn't move.

Brandon growled low. "Get your ass over here, now."

"Not until you pay." Micah stepped in front of Joni. "You want the annoying human? Give us the cash."

Brandon whispered something to his enforcers—and they suddenly lunged toward Trent, claws erupting from their fingertips.

At the same time, Brandon rushed toward Micah.

Graves had a split second to half-shift as he sprinted toward Trent. Hair sprouted from his skin, his claws extending too, and his snout elongated. In a heartbeat, he was half man, half Were.

It hurt to partially shift that fast, but he ignored the pain. Trent was outnumbered six to one. Micah could fight Brandon to hold him off. He had faith in his younger brother's fighting skills to keep Joni safe. His friend needed him more.

The enemy enforcers became five before they even reached Trent. The huge cougar came sailing from a nearby tree and brutally slammed into the sixth, taking him to the ground.

The male screamed as long claws tore into his chest. Graves saw the cougar's mouthful of sharp teeth latch onto his target's throat before blood sprayed the area.

Trent snarled, punching a male in the face with his elongated claws. One of Brandon's enforcers had frozen feet away, his gaze widening in horror as he stared at the cougar killing his now silent pack mate. Cable attacked that stupid male. The gaping idiot never saw him coming.

Graves leapt forward and landed next to Trent as the four remaining enemy enforcers tried to gang up on his friend to overwhelm him. They went back to back, slashing at Brandon's males. The enemy enforcers stumbled back at the vicious blows, showing fear at the sudden arrival of more Weres. It was clear they planned to flee.

The first one who tried to run was met by Reef, and the fight was on. A second enemy Were backed up right into Kleve.

"Go," Trent growled at Graves. "We've got them."

"No one lives," Graves snarled.

"Not a problem." Trent attacked the Were nearest him.

Graves spared a quick glance at the cougar, who sat next to dead Were, licking his bloodied claws. Jay had not only torn open the male's chest to literally rip out his heart, but his throat was mostly gone. He swore the green-eyed cougar shifter winked at him.

It would have amused him at any other time. Instead, he quickly turned his attention to his brother.

Brandon and Micah were exchanging claws and punches. The idiot alpha had his back to Graves. He seemed completely unaware of what was happening to his enforcers.

"Hey," Graves snarled. "This fucker is *mine*. Back off, Micah."

Brandon spun away from Micah. His jaw dropped and terror showed in the bastard's eyes as Graves prowled toward him.

Micah did as ordered, returning to Joni's side.

"Joni belongs to *me*. You think you can just take her? Big fucking mistake." Graves smiled when Brandon's gaze flicked to the side. He knew exactly what the man saw—Trent and his pack, taking out the rest of the trash. "It's the last mistake you'll ever make."

Graves fully expected the man to try to escape, but Brandon was a special kind of stupid.

The male yanked up his shirt and pulled a gun from his waistband.

Graves dove to the side to avoid being shot as Brandon aimed at his chest and fired.

"No!" Joni screamed.

Graves hit the ground and rolled, feeling a burning in his left arm where one of the bullets struck him. He continued moving, rolling gracefully to his feet even as more several more shots erupted.

But it wasn't Brandon firing.

He saw the male gasp and drop his gun, then he pitched forward, hitting the dirt face first.

Graves's gaze shot up and he gawked a little at Joni. She held his gun in front of her, hands steady and the weapon still trained on Brandon.

A groan came from the asshole and he planted his hands on the ground, trying to lift his body. He wasn't succeeding. His Joni had shot the son of a bitch in the back. It wouldn't kill Brandon, but it had to have fucking hurt as the bullets tore into him.

Graves stalked over to the male and bent, picking up his discarded gun. He flipped on the safety and blindly threw it toward Micah. Then he crouched a few feet away from the downed alpha, taking in the four wet spots on Brandon's clothing. Joni had hit his lower spine twice, his shoulder blade once, and nailed his left ass cheek.

Brandon whimpered as he tried to get up yet again. It was soon clear that his legs weren't working. Graves was even more impressed with Joni's shooting skills. She'd partially paralyzed him. For the moment Brandon was truly fucked. Injuries to his spinal cord could take weeks to heal...if they healed at all. He knew of at least two Were's whose legs were severely damaged thanks to spinal injuries.

He turned his head to stare at Joni. She'd finally lowered the gun, looking pale. Her gaze locked with his as she stepped toward him. Micah stopped her by gripping her shoulder with his free hand, the other holding Brandon's gun.

"Good shooting, but now he can't fight me," Graves said with a slight grin. He knew she'd done it to protect him. "I feel almost bad about killing him when he's this fucked up," he teased, letting her know he wasn't mad. "This isn't what I had in mind when I said he wasn't going to walk out of this clearing alive."

That seemed to snap her out of her shock. Joni tugged out of Micah's hold and moved forward. He tried to grab her again but she dodged his hand.

Graves motioned to his brother to let her come. Joni didn't have a violent bone in her body, and he worried about the emotional fallout of her having to kill a man. He had to know she was alright.

"You fucking cunt!" Brandon hissed, using his arms to try to crawl away from Graves. "I hate you! You ruined everything!"

"Shut the fuck up," Graves snarled.

Joni stopped feet from Graves. A pain stabbed at his chest as he saw tears well in her eyes, her body shaking.

"It's okay," he said, softening his tone. "You didn't kill him, and it was justified. He used a gun to try to take me out. You stopped him."

Graves reached for her, but when he tried to pull her close, she suddenly ducked under his arm and surprised the hell out of him by rushing toward Brandon.

He twisted, too stunned to do more than watch as Joni dropped down onto the bastard's back, straddling him.

His Joni grabbed Brandon's hair with one hand and shoved the gun into the base of his head, firing shots into his skull until the gun was empty.

Graves lunged, grabbed her, and pulled Joni off the now still male. Her grip on Brandon's hair made the body jerk as he tore her free. She released the gun and it dropped to the ground as he backed them away from Brandon, twisting her in his arms to see her face.

Her big brown eyes were still filled with tears. One slid down her pale cheek.

"Joni? What the fuck?"

More tears ran down her face. "You have too much honor to kill someone who can't fight back. So I fixed my mistake." Her voice broke. "Brandon was my problem and my responsibility. I'm tougher than you think. He *deserved* to die."

Graves didn't want to tell her that he could still hear the fucker breathing. Weres were tough to kill with bullets. It didn't mean Brandon wasn't royally screwed. His brains had to be scrambled.

He lifted his gaze to Micah. "Burn the body."

His brother glanced at Brandon before giving Graves a look. Micah could obviously hear the fucker still breathing, too.

"You heard me. Burn his body," he repeated.

His brother quickly hid his small, understanding smile. "Got it. We'll burn *all* the bodies."

Graves lifted Joni into his arms and walked away from Brandon, taking in the rest of the clearing. Cable, Reef, and Kleve were piling up the dead enforcer bodies.

Jay had disappeared, probably back into the trees, making sure the area remained secure in case someone had heard the gunfire. It would be bad if anyone came to investigate before they could clean the scene.

Trent approached him, concern on his face. "Is she okay?"

Joni wiped her face and turned her head to look at him. "I'm fine."

Graves doubted that, but he wasn't going to argue the point. "Let me spend a few minutes with Joni and then I'll help Micah load the bodies into my SUV. My pack has a crematorium we use."

"We've got it covered. No need."

That surprised Graves.

Trent smirked. "We have more friends than just you."

"Trusted ones?"

"Yes. We've got access to a local mortuary that doesn't have security cameras." Trent held his gaze. "Are we good?"

"Always. Thanks for the help. Did they bring you the rest of the money they owed?"

"No. We checked the bodies. I'll also search the vehicles they came in before we dispose of them."

"I'll pay what they owe." The pack was just starting out, they could use every cent to stay afloat.

"Just keep sending us work. We appreciate it."

Graves could definitely do that. He nodded. "I'm going to take Joni home, then."

"Good. Call if you need anything." Trent gave a sympathetic glance at Joni. The concern in his gaze proved his friend was worried about her mental state, too.

He turned but was careful to keep Joni's vision blocked from seeing Brandon. Micah gave him a nod as he approached, silently letting him know the male was no longer breathing. He'd hated putting that responsibility on his younger brother, was grateful he could handle it.

"Let's go. You're driving." Graves turned, walking out of the clearing.

Micah hurried to his side.

"I can walk." Joni wiggled against him. "You're hurt. Your arm is bleeding."

"You can bandage me up in the SUV. I'm carrying you. Deal with it." Graves wasn't willing to put her down just yet. The reality of what she'd done would hit her soon, and he wanted her to feel safe when it did. That meant holding her as close as possible.

He was glad when Joni just sighed and stilled, not arguing further.

As they walked, he debated about telling Joni the truth or not about who'd really killed Brandon. Part of him wanted to alleviate her guilt...but she'd been determined enough to take Brandon's life. Determined to protect *him*. The other part of him didn't want to take that away from her.

Graves put Joni in the backseat when they reached his SUV, grabbed the first-aid kit from the back, and tossed the keys at Micah. Then he climbed into the back with her.

"Let me see your arm," she demanded. "Is that the only place you're hurt?"

"Yes." Graves bared the wound for her, removing his shirt so she could get a good look.

The bullet had barely tagged him, since he'd moved fast enough to avoid taking a full hit. But he kept silent about that, too. It seemed to help soothe Joni as she cleaned the graze in his arm.

Chapter Fifteen

"Go shower," Graves ordered Joni as they exited the SUV. "I need to talk to Micah. I'll join you soon in my room."

Joni nodded and walked away to enter his cabin. Graves watched her go, still worried. She'd been too quiet on the drive home. Micah moved next to him, also watching her. She disappeared inside and lights came on as she closed the door.

"Why'd you let her think she killed that prick? It's better if she knows I finished him off."

"You saw what she did." Graves watched as more lights came on upstairs. "Joni was determined to be the one to kill him. That took a hell of a lot of courage. I'm not sure telling her that she failed is the best choice."

"It's better than allowing her to think she took someone's life."

Graves turned to his brother. "Is it? That asshole spent years making *her* life hell. And she grew up pack; she's seen plenty of violence. She opened fire on Brandon to stop him from shooting me full of holes. Tell me, Micah—have you ever wanted someone dead because they hurt someone you care about? Because I have. Joni dodged me, straddled the bastard, and emptied the rest of the clip into his skull to spare me from doing something she thought I'd find dishonorable."

His brother nodded. "You still would have killed him. The fucker used a gun against you. He went after someone under your protection, set up your friends, and planned to wipe out Trent's pack."

"Joni made a huge sacrifice, thinking she was doing the right thing to spare me from having to kill Brandon when he couldn't fight back. I'm not going to shit on her selfless act unless she suffers adversely. If that happens, I'll tell her the truth. For now, I'll play it by ear."

Micah sighed. "I get it." He looked away, back toward the cabin. "Dad did the same for me once. I knew about it, of course, but I still appreciated him letting me think I was the one who ended the bastard."

Graves expressed his confusion with a look at his brother.

"We never talk about the time Bufford's followers attacked our pack." Micah watched him closely.

Graves instantly flashed back to the night when his life had changed forever. He thought of the distant howls, some cut off so quickly. They were warnings from their pack mates, letting them know that something was seriously wrong. That danger had invaded their territory.

"Dad and I were outside to protect the house when some of the pack who couldn't fight fled our way. We directed them inside with Mom, so they'd be safe. Three of Bufford's bastards were chasing two females with pups clutched in their arms. The pricks were laughing, having a blast terrorizing our women."

Micah growled in memory. "Dad and I took them down. I didn't kill the one I fought, but I'd royally fucked him up. Dad dragged the bodies out of sight because more females and pups were rushing toward us, seeking shelter. I realized the bastard was still alive when I heard him whimper from behind Mom's rose bushes. Minutes later, Dad came back and told me to be proud of killing to protect our pack. It took a few years for me to realize why he didn't tell me. He wanted me to feel pride, to balance out the horror of that night. I appreciated it."

"I'm sorry I wasn't there. You were too young to be fighting at all."

"So were you. Bufford and his followers were to blame, for trying to steal our territory."

"But I was still older. I was the one who should have been standing at Dad's side to keep our family safe."

"Don't." Micah gripped his arm. "Your priority was elsewhere. Dad and I were more than enough to protect Mom from the enemies who reached us. It would have been against your nature if you hadn't gone to..."

Try to save Londa. Graves cleared his throat when his brother stopped speaking. Everyone avoided mentioning his intended mate's name. "Not that it did any good."

"You still went. It wasn't your fault that you couldn't reach her in time. Those bastards snuck into our territory right near where she lived. We never saw the attack coming. And they acted like a bunch of cowards, attacking families with claws and guns. Bufford and his followers didn't have an ounce of honor or compassion."

"I don't want to talk about this anymore." Graves *never* liked to speak of the past. The boy he'd once been had died that night with his intended mate. His grief had dulled, along with his rage over what he'd lost, but he preferred to live in the present, as the man he'd become.

"Fine. What do you think Joni's old pack is going to do, once they realize their new alpha and his enforcers must be dead?"

"I imagine someone in their pack will take over or one of the alphas bordering their territory will step in. Either way, they're better off without Brandon. Joni believed he might've eventually become a decent leader, but she was wrong. He'd have been the kind of rot that spread through his entire pack, until all of them were destroyed."

"Agreed. No pack needs that kind of alpha."

Graves reached up and squeezed his brother's shoulder. "I need to be with Joni. Thanks for the help."

"You should mate her."

Graves met his gaze, arching his eyebrow.

His brother released him and shrugged. "She killed for you. That makes Joni one hell of a woman. She's a keeper, Graves. Also, you don't terrify her. She's proud of what you do for a living, just like we are. Stop being a moron and claim her. She's yours anyway."

"Go home, and keep your mouth shut about what went down. If Mom and Dad ask, just say it's handled and Joni is safe from her old pack. Leave it at that. in fact, tell them those were my orders from Arlis. He trusted me to handle this mess and didn't want details, so they don't need them either. It's for the best. I don't want any blowback for Trent and his pack. They have enough to deal with because they're small and new."

"You got it. My lips are sealed."

As his brother left, Graves hurried toward his cabin. He entered, locked the door, and rushed up the stairs. Joni was still in the shower, her head bent under the water.

He stripped fast, making noise so he didn't startle her. She pulled back from the spray, pushed her wet hair off her face, and gave him a timid smile. He was grateful that she didn't look as if she were about to cry. He joined her in the shower and reached for the shampoo.

She glanced at his arm. "You're going to get your bandage wet."

"It's fine. It'll heal fast. The bullet barely took any flesh."

"I'm glad." She fully faced him.

"Turn back around," he ordered. "I'm going to wash your hair."

"Why?"

"You saved my life, Joni. I want to pamper you."

"In that case...let's wash *ourselves* so we're done faster and go to bed. Your bed. If you want to pamper me, I know what I want. You."

Graves muted his arousal for the moment. It was difficult to do, since he badly wanted the same thing as Joni, but he was still concerned about her mental state.

He'd used sex too many times in the past to bury his own pain, or to distract himself from facing the harsher realities of his job.

"Brandon would never have stopped coming after you." He decided to be blunt and get it out in the open, hoping to head off any guilt she might feel later for her actions. "You protected me, and that was the right thing to do."

Joni nodded, holding his gaze. "I know that."

He studied her eyes. Sincerity showed in their brown depths. He blew out a relieved breath. She really seemed okay with what she'd done, but only time would truly tell. "I'm proud of you." He pulled her into his arms, keeping their gazes locked. "You were brave and defiant and you handled the situation extremely well. I want you to know that, too."

A smile curved her lips. "You're saying I surprised you...for a human being."

"It's not just that," he admitted. "I don't think many Were women would have done anywhere near as well as you did in that situation. You let yourself become bait. Not only that, but you kept calm under extreme pressure. Own that, and know that it makes you special."

"I'm really okay, Graves." She went up on her tiptoes and wrapped her arms around his neck. "I can see that you're worried, but you don't need to be. Honest. I'd tell you if I was struggling with anything that happened. I'm good. For real." She licked her lips. "Will...will you kiss me?"

Graves didn't hesitate to lower his head and take possession of her mouth. He just hoped he was good at it, since kissing wasn't something he did—ever. For Joni, he'd learn.

Her taste and the feel of her plush mouth made his cock instantly harden to the point of pain. He growled against her lips and adjusted his hold, lifting her body to pin her against the tile. Her moan assured him that he hadn't lost his skills.

Joni wrapped her legs around his waist. It was tempting to drive his cock inside her, especially when her wet sheath rubbed against his hard-on, but he wasn't too far gone to forget that she was human. He still didn't want to risk getting Joni pregnant. The fear that he'd make a shit father hadn't changed.

Joni's hands sank into his hair as he deepened the kiss and ground his cock against her sex. Her moans increased in volume, and he broke the kiss, breathing hard. Their gazes locked. He turned, keeping hold of her and walking right out of the shower and into his bedroom.

"Condoms," he snarled, carefully dropping her on the bed so she wouldn't get hurt. He spun, frantically looking for the box. He spotted it on the nightstand and quickly grabbed one, rolling it over his dick. Joni crawled to reach the middle of his bed as he stalked closer, his gaze running over every inch of her. She spread her legs, giving him a view of how ready she was to take him.

He climbed on the bed, pinned her beneath him, and took her mouth. He liked kissing, it turned out. Her tongue matched his stroke for stroke as he adjusted his hips and used one of his hands to line them up. Then he was entering her tight sex.

He lost all control once he was inside her. Joni was *his*.

Joni tasted blood she but didn't care. Graves fucked her hard. He had her pinned under his muscled body and all she could do was feel the pleasure as he pounded into her. Her climax struck fast, and she twisted her head away from his mouth to yell out his name.

Graves buried his face against her throat, and she felt his fangs roughly scrape her skin. He didn't bite into her, but she wouldn't have cared if he did. His body shook as he came, a sexy groan filling her ear since his mouth was so close. He braced his weight a little better so both could try to catch their breaths.

"*Damn.*" Graves lifted his head, and his stormy eyes searched hers. He lowered his attention to her mouth and licked his lips, flashing his fangs, and she could see red on this tongue. "Fuck. I got you with my fangs. Open up and let me see your mouth."

"I'm okay. You just nicked my tongue. It's nothing."

"I shouldn't have lost that much control." He grimaced.

His lack of reaction surprised her. She thought he'd react with outright anger.

"I like kissing you. Minus the blood. But I don't think you'd tell me if I actually hurt you. Show me. Prove that I didn't do serious damage."

Joni stuck out her tongue, then laughed. "See? Just a little nick. I've done worse eating dinner and tagging my tongue with my dull human teeth." Her gaze fixed on his fangs, which were still showing. "My, what big canines you have." She fluttered her lashes, hoping he'd understand she was playing with him to lighten the mood. "What a big *everything* you have."

Graves smiled and lowered his body a little, still staring at her. "We need to talk."

That instantly killed her good mood. He was forever putting walls up between them. Now that Brandon was dead, it was possible that he'd try to force her to leave his pack. He'd probably use the excuse that the danger to her had been dealt with.

"Please don't send me away, Graves. I don't want to leave you." She clutched at his shoulders and tightened her hold around his waist with her legs, where they were still intimately connected. He hadn't pulled his cock out of her yet.

His expression softened. "You're staying with me. I'm done trying to send you away, I promise. That's what I wanted to talk to you about."

Relief hit hard, and her grip on him loosened slightly. "Thank you."

"I have some shit to still work through, but this is your home now."

"You won't regret it."

He took a deep breath. "What exactly do you want from me, Joni? Be honest."

Her heart pounded. "Being with you is enough. Just don't ask me to leave. I want this to be my home. For *you* to be my home."

"Why? I'm not the easiest person to be around."

"I think you're wonderful," she admitted. "I..." She decided to be brave; to just put it all out there, since he was asking. "I have...feelings for you. I didn't expect them, especially not this fast. And I know you don't want to hear that, but it's the truth."

She began to worry that she'd been *too* honest with him as long seconds passed without him saying a word. His expression didn't give her any clues to what he might be thinking.

Joni bit her lip. "I don't expect you to love me back."

His stormy blue eyes flashed with surprise. "You love me?"

She nodded.

"Damn." He adjusted his body over hers but didn't separate them. He leaned in even closer. "Okay. We're being brutally honest. I can do this..."

Joni tensed, expecting him to break her heart by confessing that he barely tolerated her, or something along those lines.

"I didn't want you here. I'm set in my ways, and forming attachments isn't something I do. Then you were suddenly in my home, and now...now I can't imagine you being gone. I look forward to coming home to you."

Tears filled her eyes. "Really?"

"Yes."

She felt pure happiness.

"I'm still too afraid to become a father. I've already mentioned why. One day, that might change, but for right now...is that okay with you? We need to get you to a doctor who can put you on something to prevent pregnancy. You were right about us Weres." He grinned. "I'd like to not have to use condoms all the time."

She frowned. "But that's..."

"Something mates should discuss before we bond."

"Mates?" She gaped at him, certain she must be hearing things.

"Mates," he repeated firmly. "But I can see you weren't prepared for me to bring that up. You obviously need more time to think about that option—"

"NO!" She clutched him tightly. "I mean, I don't need more time. *Yes.* I want to be your mate. It's just that, you said you'd never take one."

"I did." He chuckled. "Then you came into my life. Things changed."

She nodded, silently agreeing. Not once had she thought she'd fall in love with the judge her parents had gifted her to, no matter how careful their research. "I want to be your mate. Will Alpha Arlis really let you do that, though?"

"He, along with my family, are very much all in agreement that I should mate you."

Dread muted her joy. "Is that why you're offering? Because they expect it of you, since I'm your servant?"

Graves adjusted his body, cupping her face with his big hands. "Do I seem the type to do *anything* I don't want to do, just because people tell me to?"

"No."

"Damn straight." He caressed her skin. "You want brutal honesty? In a twisted way, I'm glad for all the shit Brandon pulled. It made me realize that while I never planned to let anyone get close to me, I wasn't willing to lose you." He released her face and gently withdrew his cock from her body. "Let me get rid of this condom. I'm starting to soften, thanks to all this serious shit. Be right back."

He winked and moved off her, heading to the bathroom. Joni sat up, and he returned to her quickly and climbed back onto the bed, sitting opposite her.

"I want you, Joni. Bottom line. Not as my servant. I might make a shit mate, but I'll give you my best."

She reached out, and Graves gripped her hand. "I think you'll make an amazing mate."

"I know *you* certainly will. Did your parents ever explain how it physically happens?"

"You mean actual mating?"

"Yes."

"We exchange blood during sex." Her gaze dropped to his lap. "But without a condom."

"Exactly. It's a pregnancy risk, even if you don't smell or taste like you're ovulating. But it's a risk I'm willing to take to bond with you."

She met his gaze. "I could get my tubes tied. Unlike you, my body won't heal from that kind of procedure. It will stick."

His features softened again. "Thank you for offering, but no. I'd never ask you to do that. As much as I think I'd make a terrible father."

"I don't agree with you about that. You don't give yourself enough credit. You—"

He cut her off. "You've only been in my life for a short time, so even you haven't seen me at my worst." He shrugged. "But look how much has changed already..."

He just kept surprising her. One day, she'd love to have his babies. Part of her was glad that she'd have to wait. She wanted to spend time with just him before they added to their family.

"A week ago, I couldn't imagine I'd ever want a mate." He suddenly smiled. "Maybe next month, I'll want to knock you up when you're ovulating."

Her mouth fell open and her eyes went wide.

Graves laughed and squeezed her hand. "I don't think I will, but hell, it could happen. I'm learning that you have a way of making me want things I was positive I didn't." He sobered. "It will probably be a few years, to be honest, before I'm ready for a baby, but I do want that option with you. I'm all in on this, Joni. I'm not putting limits on us or our future."

"Okay."

He got up and turned off the light, getting back into bed and pulling her into his arms. "Sleep. We'll talk more tomorrow. It's been a long day."

Joni snuggled into him. Graves held her tight, allowing her to use his chest as a pillow, his hand gently massaging her back. "I'm here if you have bad dreams. I'm never going to let anyone or anything hurt you."

"I know." She smiled in the dark, believing him. A yawn broke from her less than a minute later. She was exhausted. Sleep came quickly, but bad dreams didn't.

Chapter Sixteen

Joni shut off the water in the shower and reached for a towel, starting to dry off. She'd moved all her belongings that morning into Graves's bedroom. He'd insisted. It made her smile. He wasn't putting up walls between them anymore.

Graves had woken up earlier than her to run some errands. One of them was having breakfast with his alpha. He'd promised to give Arlis a personal update on what had happened the night before. Joni had worried that it might get Graves into trouble, but he'd assured her that wouldn't happen.

She exited the bathroom right as Graves stepped into the bedroom. She blurted out the first thing that came to mind. "How did it go? Is your alpha upset with me because my troubles followed me here?"

"No. Not at all." He smiled, his gaze raking down her body. "I told you it would be fine. Arlis and I are good. He trusts me to handle problems and doesn't blame you one bit. I wish I'd gotten home a few minutes earlier to join you in the shower." He reached for his shirt, pulling it over his head.

The sight of his bared skin had her doing a bit of staring herself. Graves was damn sexy. The wound from the night before had already healed. All that remained was a small pink mark that would fade by the next day. "I can get back in and pretend I need to wash my hair again."

He closed the distance between them and snagged her around the waist, hauling her against his front. "Just so you know, I informed him that I'm going to mate you. It was just a formality. Arlis is happy for us."

That was a huge relief. Joni ran her hands over his chest. "I think your mother is going to be thrilled when she finds out."

"That's putting it mildly. She'll want to throw a party and invite the entire pack to celebrate." His smile faded. "I'd hate that, but I'll deal if that's what you want."

"I don't need or want a party. I'd like to get to know the rest of the pack, but I'm good with doing it slowly, over time."

"Don't ever say something just because it's what you think I want to hear, Joni."

"I won't. My idea of being social was cooking for the unmated elders and enforcers, remember? They weren't exactly party people and meals usually consisted of five or six people, max."

"I'm relieved to hear that. I like to hang out with my friends and family but I hate parties. Is that bad to admit?"

"Of course not. I don't want you hiding anything from me, either."

"I won't." He eased his hold on her and stepped back, moved to the bed, and took a seat on the end of it. "Come here."

She stepped closer, watching as he removed his boots. Once he was done, he cupped her hips, spread his legs, and guided her to stand between his bare feet. Joni was curious what he was up to.

"This is a good time for me to make sure you're no longer ovulating, since you just showered. If you're not...are you willing to bond with me now? Be sure. We can't undo a mating once we exchange fluids."

Joni nodded. "I'm ready, and I'm one hundred and ten percent certain."

That made him smile. "Okay." He released her hips and tugged the towel from around her middle, tossing it into the bathroom. His large hands once again curled around her hips.

Joni gasped as Graves suddenly lifted her off her feet, twisted fast, and tossed her on the mattress. He slid off the bed, gripped her again, and pulled her to the edge of the bed.

"What are you doing?"

"The sniff and taste test." Graves winked. "Oh, and making you scream my name. That's happening too. Even if you *are* still ovulating. I'll just grab a condom if that's the case and we'll test it again tomorrow. I'm mating you as soon as it's safe."

"So *you're* sure about this?"

He held her gaze as his hands adjusted her legs so they were bent and spread, exposing her pussy to him. "I don't fuck around once I make up my mind. I'm bonding the hell out of you. Let this be a lesson..." Humor glinted in his stormy eyes. "Be careful what you wish for—or, in your case, scheme about with your parents. You wanted to belong to me? I'm keeping you forever."

Joni felt her heart melt, falling for him even more. "That was the best decision we ever made."

His expression sobered. "My birth name was Angel. I don't want any secrets between us. I'm not the kid I used to be. I'm Graves now. I just wanted you to know."

She smiled. "Thank you for trusting me with that, Graves."

He leaned back and looked down. "Damn, I'm hard already. You're beautiful, Joni." He licked his lips and bent over her.

His hot breath fanned her thighs. Graves didn't tease. He inhaled, and a low growl came from him. "I don't smell you ovulating. Now let me taste..." He spread her wider and ran his tongue over her clit.

Joni grabbed at the comforter to avoid pulling his hair. Pleasure and excitement had her moaning his name as he began to torment her. She *loved* oral sex. Graves had shown her just how amazing it could be with his mad skills. Her climax built fast and broke.

"Not ovulating." Graves lifted his head and climbed on the bed, his voice gruff. "I'm going to take you bare, fill you with my seed, but before I do..." He stared deeply into her eyes.

She waited anxiously for him to continue.

"I'll use my claws to cut my shoulder. Then I'll bite you right before I come. Drink my blood while I fuck you. Do you understand? Drink as much as you can. That's how we bond as mates."

"I will."

"Good." He grabbed her hips and yanked her closer. Then he slowly entered her.

Joni moaned as his thick cock stretched her pussy when he sank deep. She thought he couldn't feel any better than he had before, but there was a difference without the condom. He felt bigger and hotter.

When he started to move, she lost the ability to think.

"*Fuck*," he rasped. "So damn good, baby! I'm not going to last long."

She wasn't going to either, her second climax already building as he picked up speed, pounding into her. He reached up and she saw that his claws were out. Part of her hated to see him slice open his skin, but knowing why he created the wound made it more exciting. She was becoming his mate.

He fucked her harder, leaned forward to pin her tightly under him, and his mouth went for her neck. "Drink," he snarled.

Joni kissed his shoulder where he bled. Just as the coppery taste on her tongue registered, Graves bit her, his fangs breaking the skin.

She cried out from the pain, but also from the pleasure. Her body was confused but it didn't matter. She climaxed, swallowing her mate's blood as it filled her mouth.

Graves's body jerked violently over hers as he came, his hot semen filling her. Joni's mother had explained that the blood exchange during sex triggered changes in a Werewolf's semen, marking a female by scent so others knew she belonged to him. The more they did it, the stronger the scent—and the bond—would become.

They clung together, bodies trembling, for what seemed like hours. Graves licked at her bite, nuzzling her. "Mine," he rasped next to her ear.

"You're mine too."

"Damn straight, and never forget it."

"I won't," she vowed.

They made love slower the next round, and Graves had them exchange more blood. They were catching their breaths when his phone started to ring.

Graves cursed, moving away from her to retrieve his pants that had ended up on the floor. Joni didn't even remember him taking them off. He'd probably done it when he'd been going down on her.

"I have to get this. It could be important. I'm always on call."

"I know. It's okay."

He met her gaze as he lifted the phone to his ear. "Graves here." He listened to whoever had called. "Yeah. Got it. I'll see you later today." He ended the call.

Joni slid off the bed. "I'll start the shower for you if you want to grab some clothes. How fast do you have to leave, and any idea how long you'll be gone? I'll miss you, but…" She forced a smile. "I'll be here when you get back. Just be careful. I never want to lose you."

Graves grabbed her, pulling her against him. "That wasn't work. It was my dad. Mom is driving him nuts because she wants to make sure you're safe and unharmed after I allowed you to be bait. I'm not her favorite son today. We've been invited to dinner, and he warned that if we don't show up there, she'll be coming here and breaking in if we don't answer the door."

Joni was glad he wasn't leaving her so soon after they'd mated. "Your mom wouldn't have to break in. She still has the spare key you gave her. That's how she got in yesterday."

His expression was pained. "I never gave her one. Mom somehow keeps sneaking my keys and making copies. I'm going to have to change the locks—*again*. That's like the fifth time in two years."

That cracked Joni up. "I love your mom."

"She's a menace." He shook his head. "But I love her too. I should warn you, though. You're not officially one of her kids until she's trying to guilt you into giving her grandbabies. Don't let her bully you."

"I think I can handle it." She went up on her tiptoes and slid her arms around his neck. "I didn't let *you* bully me, and you're way more intimidating than your mom. I'm still here."

He kissed her lips, holding her tighter. "I'm thankful that you stood up to me. It's one of the things that made me love you so fast."

Joy spread through her chest. He'd admitted that he loved her! She wasn't going to point it out. Graves was the kind of guy who needed time to adjust to new things or he'd freak out a little. Or a lot. Instead, she just smiled. "I'm no pushover."

"I know."

His phone went off again.

"Damn!"

Joni released him. "Like you said, you're always on call. This is what you do, and I knew that before we ever met. I don't want you to change. You're exactly the man I fell in love with."

He retrieved his cell and answered. "Graves. What do you need?"

He listened. That time, his features harshened. "How many?" Seconds ticked by. "That's bad. I agree." He went silent, watching her as whoever had called spoke again. "You know what? Call the clans. I just got mated, so I'm taking a few weeks off to celebrate. The VampLycans or GarLycans will help you out." He winked at Joni. "Thanks. Good luck with your nest problem." He ended the call.

"You don't have to take time off."

"I want to."

Joni threw herself at him. "Thank you!"

"I'm your mate. I take that seriously, Joni. We need time to strengthen our bond. That means me not taking on every job that comes my way. Some things, the clans can deal with. My constant urge to stay busy is already subsiding, now that I know you're here in our home." His stormy gaze locked with hers. "I finally feel grounded again. *You've* given me that."

It was so sweet that she blinked back tears. "Good. I don't expect you to change though. I'm just putting that out there."

"Okay. We—"

Boom!

Graves quickly clamped his hand over her mouth. "Lock yourself in the bathroom," he demanded, his voice so low she barely heard the words. He released her a heartbeat later and moved toward his bedroom door.

There was a loud snarl from the first floor. Someone was inside the cabin.

Joni ran into the bathroom but it wasn't to follow orders. Instead, she grabbed a towel to wrap around her middle. Her gaze skimmed the counter for a weapon and she quickly decided on the mug Graves used as a toothbrush holder. It was a pathetic choice, but there were no other options.

She spun, rushing out of the bedroom to follow Graves. Her mind was a jumble of suspicions. It could be someone from her old pack who suspected she was somehow to blame for Brandon's disappearance. Then again...Graves did make a lot of enemies being a judge.

Joni reached the top of the stairs in time to see Graves launch himself toward the kitchen. He'd half-shifted, fur, claws, and fangs on display.

"It's me! Don't attack!"

It took a second to recognize the male's voice. She hurried down the stairs as Graves started to rant.

"What the fuck, Dad? Why are you on the laundry room floor? Hell, why are you in my *cabin*?"

"Can you stop glaring at me, cover your dick, and help me up? I climbed through the window, got stuck because it's a damn small opening, and while trying to wiggle free, I fell. I hit the top of your machines, slid off, and now my foot is stuck between your washer and dryer."

"Why are you even here? Why didn't you just knock if you wanted to speak to me?"

"You know your mother. She didn't want to wait until dinner to make sure Joni was okay. I went to take a piss, came out, and she was gone. I figured she'd come straight here. She has a spare key again but you tend to change the locks, so if the key didn't work, her backup plan was breaking your laundry window latch. I figured I'd get here first, grab her, and take her back home before you even realized she was in the house."

"Goddamn it," Graves sighed. "She's not here. Give me a moment to put on pants. You're really do look stuck."

"No shit." His father winced. "My leg is wedged in there tight."

Joni had stayed at the bottom of the stairs, and she struggled not to laugh. Graves quickly rushed from the kitchen, his body shifting back to human form as he approached. Their gazes locked—then he glanced at the mug in her hand and growled.

"I wanted to help."

He came to a halt in front of her. "Were you planning to get me some water to drink after I kicked the intruder's ass?"

"I was going to throw it. It's the first thing I saw," she admitted. "I didn't know what was going on."

"I told you to lock yourself up."

"And *I* said I wanted to help," she repeated.

"Fuck. We're going to talk about this later, but not now." He took the mug, stepped around her, and jogged up the stairs.

Joni admired his bare ass until he was out of sight, then she tentatively headed toward the laundry room, hoping Angelo wasn't pantless again. The sight of him had her struggling again not to laugh. She figured it would be rude.

Graves's father wore sweatpants and a tank top—thank God—as he lay sprawled on the floor. One leg was indeed pinned in the space between the two big machines. The was bent at a weird angle because of the way he was trapped.

Angelo twisted his head to look at Joni and gave her a rueful smile. "Hi. Sorry about this. So Mandy really isn't here?"

"Nope." She moved closer to get a better view of his predicament. The washer and dryer were spaced a few inches apart, but sandwiched between two walls on either side in the tight space. The window above them was open where he'd entered the cabin. Graves would probably have to lift one of the machines to free him. "Are you in pain?"

"No. Just a bit embarrassed. I thought I could sneak in, grab my mate, and get her out of here. I saw the SUV parked in front, but didn't hear my son yelling, so..." He sighed. "I was *sure* this is where she snuck off to."

"We haven't seen her."

"Figures. That woman drives me nuts!"

Graves had put on his jeans when he returned seconds later, gently bumped Joni out of his way, and entered the cramped laundry room. "You *both* drive me nuts." He spread his feet apart to avoid stepping on his dad, leaned against the washing machine, and grabbed Angelo's foot. "I don't want to lift the machine and risk dropping it on your head. This might hurt. It'll serve you right."

"I was just trying to keep anyone from disturbing you."

"Good job with that," Graves snorted.

Joni lost it then, giggling. She put her hand over her mouth to muffle the sound.

Graves twisted his head to glance at her, looking completely put out. It only made it funnier.

He turned his attention back to his father, adjusting his body to press tightly against the washer. "On three, I'm yanking your leg out. One. Two. Three!"

It worked. Graves got his father free and backed out of the laundry room as Angelo slowly stood. "You're both banned from my cabin for at least a month. Seriously! This breaking-in shit is getting old."

"It's not breaking in if you leave your keys where I can copy them. It's your own fault for giving me the opportunity to get one over on you," Mandy argued, suddenly appearing in the kitchen. Joni jumped, startled. "Call it payback for all the times you stole cookies and other sweets from my kitchen while you were growing up."

Joni gaped at Graves's mother. "I didn't even hear you come in."

"I'm skilled like that. Angelo, what are you doing here?"

"I wasn't wrong, after all. She *is* here." Angelo exited the laundry room and strode toward his mate. "Coming after you."

Someone pounded on the front door.

"We're moving to Siberia," Graves muttered, shooting a dirty look at his parents as he stomped to the door, throwing it open.

Micah waited on the other side. "Mom has ordered me to get you out of the cabin so she can speak with Joni alone. Just a heads-up."

"You're a terrible son," Mandy called out. "I said *help* me. Not tattle."

Micah stepped inside the cabin, spotting his parents. "Shit."

"You got our other son involved in your shenanigans? Mandy..." Angelo sounded disappointed.

"Enough," Graves ordered. "Everyone but Joni—get out!"

"Come on." Angelo grabbed his mate, steering her toward the front door. "He's not going to agree to have dinner with us if you piss him off enough. Pick your battles, mate. Joni is fine. I *told* you that."

"Wait!" Mandy struggled to break free, her gaze fixed on Joni. "Oh my!" Mandy used one of her hands and shoved Joni's hair away from her neck. "You're bitten! Does that mean what I think it does? Say it's so, Graves!"

His mother, his father, *and* Micah all inhaled deeply, trying to scent her, as Graves got between his parents and Joni. "We mated. You'd have found that out later, in a better way, if you—"

"This is the best news *ever*!" Mandy elbowed her mate but he managed to keep ahold of her. "Let me hug my new daughter."

"No. You'll make her lose her towel." Graves growled, moving to Joni's side and putting his arm around her. "We'll come to dinner, but for right now, get out. Or I swear...Siberia," he threatened again.

"We're going." Angelo lifted his mate, tossing her over his shoulder. "Dinner is at five."

Mandy used her hands to shove her upper body higher, grinning at Joni and Graves. "I have an official daughter! We'll throw a party. I'll invite—"

"No," Graves yelled. "No parties. Just dinner. Family only."

"I hear you," Angelo called out. "I'll keep her in line. Micah, get the door."

"Welcome to the family, Joni." Micah held the door as his father carried his mother outside, before following and firmly closing it after them. "You finally got smart, big brother. Great job!" he shouted from outside.

Graves sighed, turning to peer down at her. "I'm sorry that my family is nuts."

Joni started laughing and snuggled into his chest. "I love them—and you."

He grumbled as he hugged her back. "That makes you crazy, too. so at least you'll fit right in."

Warmth spread through her chest. She really did belong with Graves. "I'm happy about that."

He studied her face, his stormy gaze serious. "I'm happy that you forced your way into my life. I fought it at first but you're too irresistible. Thank you, Joni." He leaned in to brush his lips against hers. "We're going to be happy, baby."

"I know." She had absolute faith in that.

About the Author

NY Times and USA Today Bestselling Author

I'm a full-time wife, mother, and author. I've been lucky enough to have spent over two decades with the love of my life and look forward to many, many more years with Mr. Laurann. I'm addicted to iced coffee, the occasional candy bar (or two), and trying to get at least five hours of sleep at night.

I love to write all kinds of stories. I think the best part about writing is the fact that real life is always uncertain, always tossing things at us that we have no control over, but when writing you can make sure there's always a happy ending. I love that about being an author. My favorite part is when I sit down at my computer desk, put on my headphones to listen to loud music to block out everything around me, so I can create worlds in front of me.

For the most up to date information, please visit my website. www.LaurannDohner.com

Made in United States
Orlando, FL
29 December 2023